Arranged Love

By

P.G.Van

© 2018 P.G. Van

All rights reserved. No part of this publication may be reproduced, distributed, or transmitted in any form or by any means, including photocopying, recording, or other electronic or mechanical methods, without prior written permission of the author.

This is a work of fiction. Names, characters, businesses, places, events and incidents are either the product of the author's imagination or used in a fictitious manner. Any resemblance to actual persons, living or dead, or actual events is purely coincidental.

Blurb

Nivri does not enjoy flying alone—she hates it but gets on a plane from New York to India to surprise her family for Diwali. What she never expected were the surprises life would throw her in the short time she is in India.

Starting with spending an adventurous thirty-six hours with a complete stranger who soon turns unforgettable. Like her favorite song she couldn't stop humming, she cannot stop thinking about him.

Nivri is amazed by the strong feelings she has developed for a complete stranger. Will she follow her heart and trust her feelings to be love for a man she met in her travels?

Arranged Love is a short and sweet story about how life gives Nivri love as her surprise. It ends with a sweet happily ever after.

Chapter 1

"Thank you, Dr. Fong. I appreciate you letting me take my mid-terms sooner." Nivri smiled at her professor.

"No problem. Hope you enjoy your time with family." The older woman smiled at her graduate assistant.

"What would you like from India?" Nivri beamed.

"Oh, you know what I want and be sure to be back before your finals." Her professor issues a friendly warning.

"Yes, I do. Your favorite Laddus. It's festival season coming up in India, so they make special ones during this time." She laughed.

"Hey, are you getting married on this trip?" her professor asked surprising Nivri.

Nivri shook her head. "No way, why do you ask?"

"That's been the trend with people who go to India mid-semester."

"Not at all. I am going back home to spend Diwali with my grandma... she hasn't been in good health, and this year my dad is planning a huge celebration in our ancestral village. My family doesn't know I am going... it's a surprise, so there is no way I am getting married."

"That's wonderful news. I'd hate to lose a good graduate assistant." Dr. Fong smiled making Nivri beam at her.

"Thank you, Dr. Fong."

"Safe travels and hope you have a good time."

"Thank you. I will submit my graduate thesis from India." Nivri waved to her professor and walked away with a wide grin on her face. She couldn't wait to see the surprise on her grandma's face when she shows up in their ancestral village.

Nivri had not planned to go until a few days ago. Her grandma had sounded so dejected on the phone when Nivri told her she couldn't be home for Diwali. The next day, she put in a request with her professor and booked her long flight back home for her favorite holiday, the festival of lights.

Later that day, Nivri sat at the airport gate dreading the long flight but excited about going home. It was the first time she was returning after being away from her family for almost two years. Her parents visited a year ago during her winter break, and she was going to take a break after her graduation in a couple of months, but she felt compelled to make this trip.

She looked around the waiting area trying to gauge how full the flight was going to be, and based on the people around her, she was hopeful she would be able to skip sitting in the window seat. She was so excited she even found a seat, she booked the flight before checking if the seat was what she preferred. It was too late to change it by the time she realized it was a window seat, and all she could hope was to have a friendly seat neighbor. It wasn't really about how friendly the people she was going to be sitting next to was, but the idea of sitting in the window seat made her want to vomit—the very thought making her feel claustrophobic.

When the boarding announcement was made, she was one of the first ones to board right behind the seniors and found the row of her assigned seat and sat in the aisle seat. She counted on her good vibes that no one would show up to claim the seat she was in. Her hopes went up when the plane filled up, and no one stopped at her row.

Nivri was so confident no one was going to claim the seat she was in, she smiled victoriously to herself looking at the empty window seat. She strapped on the seat belt and plugged in the headphones to enjoy her first movie on the eighteen-hour flight from New York to India. She knew she would fall asleep halfway through the movie from staying up the past few nights studying for her mid-terms.

Nivri's seat was just warming up, the opening titles on the movie had just started to show on the screen when she realized someone was approaching her. She raised her eyes and had to tilt her head up to look the tall person in the eyes.

Dark brown eyes locked with hers, and she blinked taking in an image of the tall man who stood, looking down at her, one edge of his mouth twisted up. She took off her headphones and looked at him in silence.

"You are in my seat," he said, opening the luggage compartment above them to stow his bag away.

Nivri looked up at him and gave him her friendliest smile. "I'm sorry, I…" her words drifted when another man approached them.

"Nash, I got you an aisle seat, mine is all the way at the back." The man hurried to the back of the plane.

Nivri was still smiling and looked at the man who seemed to be patiently waiting for her to get out of his way. "I… I suffer from claustrophobia… can I please sit in your seat?"

"You're kidding." He smirked.

"Please, at least till we take off?" she whispered.

The man looked at her for a long moment and nodded. "Sure."

"Thank you, thank you!" She almost squealed with happiness and watched the tall and broad figure fit into the seat next to her that had looked tiny even for her to sit. The generous man was tall and quite good looking, or did he appear to be so because of his kindness? She was going to take it one step at a time, take-off first. And maybe she could spend most of the time walking or hanging out with the air hostesses, spend some time in the bathroom—strike that. She planned to walk around until she was ready to pass out and only wake up when they were about to land in New Delhi.

"The last time I sat by the window, I was seven," the man said as he put on his seat belt.

"Thank you, I know it is very inconvenient for you but..." her voice trailed off feeling guilty about making a man way taller than her squeeze into *her* seat.

"Only for the takeoff," he said, his knees pushing against the seat in front of them.

"Yes, thank you." Nivri knew there was no way she could sit in the window seat for more than ten minutes. If only she had paid attention to her seat number while booking her ticket.

"You are welcome." He smiled, his eyes scanning her face, lazily.

Nivri smiled looking at him gratefully before looking away to continue watching her movie. She put on her headphones and shut her eyes, blocking out the bile that threatened to rise as the plane started to pick up speed. She was never a fan of flying, and the turbulence made her very nervous. If she could drive across continents, she would make it a road trip rather than fly.

Chapter 2

The humming noise brought Nivri out of her suspended state. The space around her was dimly lit, and it took her a few seconds to remember where she was. When it all came to her, she realized her cheek was pressed against something soft, and she was in a very comfortable position. She blinked a few more times and realized her face was inches from a screen.

Startled, she lifted her head to look at where her head was resting. To her surprise, a couple of small airplane pillows were bundled together in a blanket and were placed on the tray table—not hers but the one next to her. She sat back slowly looking at the man whose head was pressed back onto the window, his eyes shut tight, his body turned to one side so that he could stretch his legs.

Nivri bit her lip, partly embarrassed by how she had passed out and woke up leaning over a stranger's tray table. It was almost like she was sleeping with her head in his lap. She looked down at her legs, almost rubbing against his stretched ones and pulled her feet up on to the seat. She wasn't short but not tall either and sometimes found the seats on the airplanes extremely tight. She felt guilty about making a man who was at least half a foot taller than her squeeze into the tight space when he could have stretched his legs out, comfortably. She looked at him in the dim light, and he seemed to be fast asleep to wake him to give his seat back.

She looked at her watch and realized she had been sleeping for almost eight hours. She stood up happy she was almost halfway through the flight and walked to the bathroom. She stepped into the bathroom dreading the feeling of being in a closed space and managed to get out of it quickly before she vomited.

Nivri asked the air hostess for water and headed back to her seat to find the man awake, and he had straightened back to sitting normally. She smiled sheepishly as she walked back, her eyes on him.

"I'm sorry, I passed out like that. You can have your seat back." Nivri looked at him, standing by the seat.

"You can have the seat. I'm fine here." His tone was flat, and she couldn't figure out if he were kidding.

"Are you sure?" she asked almost not wanting to.

"Yes, looks like you need that seat more than I do." He smiled.

"I appreciate it... please don't hesitate to wake me up if you need to use the restroom or stretch." Nivri settled back into her seat and put on her seat belt.

The man chuckled and shook his head.

Nivri was confused. "Something I said is funny?"

He smiled looking at her. "In the past few hours, I tried to wake you up twice but..."

Nivri didn't let him finish. "I'm so sorry... the past few nights I've been up preparing for my mid-terms and didn't get much sleep." She was so embarrassed she looked away unable to look him in the eye.

"That's fine. I just managed to get out and get in without having to disturb you." He laughed, putting her at ease.

"I'm so sorry for the trouble."

"What were you studying for?"

"Mid-terms... master's program." She smiled at him.

"What are you mastering?" His tone was playful.

"Business administration."

"What is your..." He was interrupted by his friend who she had seen before the flight took off.

"Nash, I need you to review and approve this, and then we will be all set. I won't bother you again for the rest of the flight." The man sounded impatient as he placed a laptop in front of the man sitting next to her.

"Now?" the man almost growled.

"Yes, Nash. Please. I am planning to take time off for the upcoming festivals. I need to take care of it," the man's friend insisted.

"Okay. I'll review it and add my notes. Give me thirty minutes."

When the man's friend left, he looked at the computer screen for a few minutes. Nivri heard him type, and less than ten minutes later, he put the laptop away and looked at her.

"By the way, I'm Avinash." He held his hand out.

"I'm Nivri... nice to meet you, Avinash. Actually, Nash is a cool name," she said remembering how his friend had addressed him.

"Yeah, most of my friends call me Nash."

"Are you working on the plane?"

"Not really... just taking care of a few things before we all take time off for Diwali."

"That's nice... I'm going back home for Diwali, too," she said, getting excited about seeing her family.

"How long has it been since you've been home?"

"Almost two years, but it has been five years since I celebrated Diwali with my family. I'm excited." She glowed with happiness.

"Are you graduating soon?" His voice was soft.

"Yes, in December. What do you do?" she asked, suddenly curious about what Avinash and his friend were talking about.

"I work in technology."

"Oh. Your boss makes you work on a plane?" She smiled.

"Part of the perks of owning your own company."

"Nice. What do you make?"

"I don't want to give you the tech spiel, but let's just say we make medical equipment for hospitals."

"For hospitals in India?" She turned to look at him.

"Of course."

"Do you operate from New York?"

He smiled shaking his head. "A hospital in New York wanted to work with us to obtain our equipment."

"Wow, that's amazing."

"How often do you travel to New York?"

"Not a lot, but I think we will make a few trips in the..." His voice trailed off when he saw his friend approach them.

"Nash, we are going to lose connectivity shortly. We need you to sign that contract now." His friend was insistent.

"Prahaas, I need you to calm down." Avinash had a smile on his face, but that didn't seem to calm his friend.

15

"I can't... do it now," Prahaas almost growled.

"Sure. Oh, Prahaas, meet Nivri. Nivri, this is Prahaas, my friend from college and business partner."

Prahaas seemed to relax, and he smiled at Nivri. "Nice to meet you, Nivri."

"Same here, Prahaas. I was planning to walk around the cabin to stretch my legs. Please feel free to sit here if you need to work together," Nivri said, standing up.

As she stood up, she heard a muffled objection from Avinash, but Prahaas was quick to take the offer. "Thank you! We only need five minutes."

"Take your time," she said and walked toward the front of the cabin smiling at the group of air hostesses talking to each other. She stood by the cabin door looking out of the window, thrilled to see the expression on her grandma's face when she sees her in their ancestral home. Her grandma lived in the village where she was born, and Nivri was going to go directly to her grandma instead of stopping in her hometown to travel with her parents after a few days.

She took a deep breath dreading the rest of the flight journey and the connecting flight. If she had time, she would have probably driven all the way from New Delhi to where her grandma lived in a rural part of South India.

Nivri was lost in thought and had not realized the captain had turned on the seat belt signal. The ground under her feet shook sending a shiver up her spine. The worst part of the plane ride was starting, and she wasn't sitting.

Flashes of the accident played in front of her eyes as she started walking back to her seat, her legs trembling.

Chapter 3

Nivri hurried back to her seat, holding her breath, the fear associated with the turbulence surrounding her threatening to suck her into the darkness.

"Prahaas, I need to sit down." She stood next to her seat clinging to the seat in front of her as Prahaas got out of her seat, a shocked expression on his face.

Nivri settled into the seat, her body shivering from the turbulence.

"Nivri, are you okay?" Avinash asked as she frantically put on her seat belt.

"I can't talk right now." Nivri hid her face in her hands and leaned forward.

Avinash reached for the air sickness bag and handed it to her and looked at his friend. "Prahaas, go get her some water."

Nivri pushed away the water that Prahaas offered and looked up at Avinash. "Just leave me alone… I will be fine."

Avinash took the glass of water from Prahaas and nodded at him.

"I'll send the contract, Nash," Prahaas mumbled as he turned to leave.

Avinash looked at the woman sitting next to him shivering like a frightened rabbit. He didn't know what to do or say. She sat in her seat, her knees drawn into her chest, her arms wrapped around her, looking like she saw a ghost.

"Nivri." His voice was a whisper, but she turned to look in his direction but not into his eyes. He placed the stack of pillows she had slept on earlier on the tray table and patted on the pillows.

Nivri shook her head and looked up at him, a film of water in her eyes. "I hate this part."

Avinash looked at her feeling compelled to help and also helpless at the same time. He leaned closer to her and asked softly. "How can I help?"

She looked up into his eyes and blurted, "Hold me… just put your arms around me."

Avinash hesitated for a moment before sliding the seat divider up and running his arm around her shoulder and pulling her close to him. The moment her cheek touched his chest, she wound her arms around him tightly, shivering from the shuddering of the plane.

The turbulence was getting better, but Nivri was still dealing with the aftereffect, enveloped in the warmth of a complete stranger's embrace. It was the first time she was traveling by herself and never felt so shaken up. She felt relieved and embarrassed as she steadied her breathing, her fingertips digging into his hard flesh. She took in the musky smell of his cologne, and the masculine scent somehow put her at ease.

Nivri loosened her hold around him and pulled away to look at him. "Thank you... I..."

"It's okay. Do you want some water?" He handed her the cup of water which she took gratefully.

"Thank you so much... I hate planes...flying for this very reason."

"I've never met someone who hates planes so much." He smiled.

"I had a very bad experience on the plane when I was little."

"Oh, what happened?" Avinash twisted his body slightly to rest his back on the wall of the plane.

"Accident... I was eight years old, and we were traveling as a family. The pilot lost control of the plane, and we had to crash-land on fields. Everyone got away with minor bruising, but my grandpa... he had a condition that caused internal bleeding from the impact and..."

"I'm sorry." He placed his hand over hers, gently.

"He was sitting right next to me... he was holding my hand as he walked out and suddenly, he collapsed." She sniffled.

"That's sad. How long ago was this?"

"Almost fifteen years ago. I was eight, and I remember everything... my grandpa was the one comforting me, and just when I thought I was invincible as long as my grandpa was around, he..." She fought back tears.

Avinash patted her hand and gave her the glass of water. "Finish the water."

Nivri smiled at him. "This is the first time I am traveling by myself. I usually have a friend or my parents with me."

"Where are you headed from New Delhi?"

"Bangalore."

"Oh, I am going to Bangalore as well."

Nivri smiled, relief sweeping over her face. "Oh good. Thank you for being so nice. I will let you get back to work. Wake me up if you need to stretch your legs or use the restroom."

"Sure." Avinash smiled as she placed the rolled-up pillows on her tray table and went back to sleep. He pulled out his computer and was thankful the Wi-Fi in the flight was still on.

Avinash fired up his Messenger and saw Prahaas was online.

Avinash: *Hey, I need to go to Bangalore from New Delhi.*

Prahaas: *What? But we have the reunion planned in Hyderabad.*

Avinash: *I need to be on the same plane Nivri is taking to Bangalore. Make sure I am sitting next to her.*

Prahaas: *Seriously?*

Avinash: *Yes.*

Prahaas: *You don't want to take the jet to Bangalore. I can fly commercial.*

Avinash: *No, you take the jet to Hyderabad. I need to go to Bangalore.*

Prahaas: *Need to?*

Avinash: *I want to... make it happen.*

Prahaas: *Yes, boss.*

Avinash: *Thank you!*

Avinash's eyes scanned the face of the beautiful woman as she tried to fall asleep. The pink in her cheeks had returned, and a small smile played on her lips. When he saw her sitting in his seat, his heart rate sped up, and something stirred deep inside him. She had a 'touch me not' manner about her and never expected her to share something so personal with him. He saw the relief on her face when he told her he was on the same plane as hers to Bangalore, and that look on her face made him feel warm inside his chest— a feeling he was starting to like a lot.

Chapter 4

"Congratulations, ma'am, your seat has been upgraded, and yes, it is an aisle seat." The woman behind the airline counter smiled at her, handing the new boarding pass to Nivri at the New Delhi airport.

"Thank you so much." Nivri looked at Avinash, who stood less than a foot from her and added, "Do you know where you are sitting?"

Avinash stepped closer and smiled at the woman. "Could you please give my friend and me seats next to each other?"

Avinash smiled to himself enjoying the way Nivri beamed at him when the airline employee told her their seats were together. He took the bag she was holding as she put her boarding pass in her purse.

"I'm so glad we are sitting next to each other. I thought you would be spooked if I asked for a seat next to you. Thank you for asking."

Avinash smiled at her. "I need you to stop thanking me for everything."

"Fine... friends?" She held her hand out, and he took in the softness of her palm as he shook her hand.

"Would you like to eat something?" he asked as they walked toward the stores and restaurants.

"Yes, I am starving, and I'm buying." She smiled. It was almost eight in the morning, and they had a couple of hours before their flight to Bangalore.

"Sure." Avinash followed her into one of the restaurants at the airport terminal.

"Where do you live in Bangalore?" she asked as they sat down and saw a surprised look on his face.

"I... I don't live there... I am going there for a meeting."

"Oh, and Prahaas is not going with you?" she asked, scanning the menu.

"No, he had to go to Hyderabad."

"Oh, I'm from Hyderabad. That's where my parents live."

Avinash frowned. "And you are going to Bangalore?"

She smiled putting away the menu and making eye contact with the waiter. "I'm visiting my grandma first. She is in our ancestral village which will take me four hours by car."

Avinash smiled and looked at the waiter who approached their table. "I'll have a coffee, please."

"Avinash, you should eat something. It's a four-hour flight to Bangalore."

"I'll eat later." He smiled and looked at her in surprise as she ordered almost everything on the menu. She wasn't thin but small compared to his structure, and the food she was ordering was for two men his size.

"You really are hungry." He observed.

"Yes. I haven't eaten since the morning I boarded the plane in New York."

"And you are going to eat everything you order before you board another plane?"

"I never throw up on the plane. I just have panic attacks, plus the route this flight takes is less turbulent."

"Interesting... you know all that?"

"I have to. Every flight I board I check high-pressure points on the route."

"I do not know anyone who does that." He shook his head smiling.

"Now you do... how long are you in Bangalore?"

"Umm... a few days. How about you?"

"I will be in India for almost three weeks. I will make a trip to Hyderabad if I have time, and if not, I'm heading back to New York."

"You are traveling back alone?" he raised a curious eyebrow.

"Yes, unless you want to accompany me," she said, playfully making him laugh. "Jokes apart, do call me when you are in New York. I will take you out for dinner."

"Are you asking me out? Do you think I'm single?" he teased.

"No... you can bring your significant other if..." Her voice trailed off when he started laughing.

"It's so easy to get you frazzled. I would love to go out with you. Are you single?"

She blushed making him grin. "Yes. No time to date. School is crazy."

"Good. I will definitely call you when I'm in New York if you give me your phone number."

"Sure... I'll text you my number. What's yours?"

They exchanged phone numbers, and her food started to arrive. A teenage boy brought them their food, and he saw Nivri's expression shift.

"You are too young to be working here." Nivri looked at the boy as he served the food on the table.

"I don't work here. I am just helping. My mother works in the kitchen."

"You are up early," she chatted with the boy as he placed the dishes on the table.

"My mom works the early shift on a few days. I didn't want to stay home alone to study. I am studying in the back."

"What grade are you in?" Nivri continued to probe.

"I am in ninth grade."

"Do you do a good job in school?"

"Yes, but... I..."

"What?"

"The kids in my class get into trouble all the time, and they keep disturbing me when I am trying to study. I want to be a doctor when I grow up." The teenage boy continued to talk, surprising Avinash.

"Which school would you like to go to?"

The young boy turned and looked at the back of the restaurant. "I want to study in the English school, but my mother tells me I have to go to..."

"What is your name?" Nivri asked gesturing the boy to sit next to Avinash.

"Raju."

"Raju, can you give your mother a phone number and have her call that number?"

"Why?"

"When you call that phone number, they will check your grades and school, and if you are doing well, they will help you go to the school you like." Nivri smiled.

The kid looked at her suspiciously before turning to look at the kitchen entrance and back at Nivri. "For real?"

"Yes." Nivri wrote a phone number on a piece of napkin and gave it to the boy.

"When can I call?" The boy seemed eager.

"Call in exactly ten minutes," Nivri said, taking her phone out of her pocket.

Chapter 5

Avinash watched her, sipping his coffee as she made a few phone calls. She spoke on the phone for a few minutes and instructed someone about expecting a call from Raju's mother and having Raju enroll in the program.

Nivri ended her call and dipped her spoon into the couple of dishes she had ordered, her eyes rolling to the back of her head as she enjoyed the first bite of each dish.

"Were you serious about what you told that kid?" Avinash asked.

She nodded, chewing on her food.

"Who did you call?" Avinash was intrigued.

"I called the person who can help Raju." She licked the tip of her finger.

"And who is that?"

"The head of the foundation which sponsors education for underprivileged kids with the eagerness to study."

"I'm impressed."

She smiled, chewing her food. "Really?"

"Yes. Do you like the food?" He smiled.

"Yes, but my favorite food is what my grandma makes... I can't wait to see her for dinner." Nivri's eyes lit up.

"Will you call me if you visit Hyderabad? I would like to take you out for dinner."

"Are *you* asking me out?" She laughed, but he looked at her for a long moment, his expression unfaltering.

"Yes, I would like to take you out on a date." His voice was soft, yet steady.

Nivri smiled. "You still want to go on a date after seeing me freak out like that on the plane?"

"Why not? I think you are interesting, and I'd like to know more about you."

"Okay. We can go out in New York even if I can't make it to Hyderabad on this trip." She smiled, suddenly feeling her cheeks heat up.

"We can have dinner in Bangalore. My meeting is not until tomorrow," Avinash suggested.

"Sorry, buddy. As I said, I have a date with my grandma tonight." She laughed making him smile.

"I'll take you out on a date before you leave town... I can't wait until I see you in New York," he said, making her breath hitch.

A few hours later...

"Ladies and gentlemen, this is the captain speaking..."

Nivri blinked open her eyes to the distant voice and started listening to the words, but she could not follow what the announcement was about. She looked around and saw the same questioning look on the other passenger's faces. She turned to look to her left, and Avinash was sleeping with his head resting against the window.

She stopped one of the flight attendants who was rushing to the front of the airplane and asked her about the announcement.

"Ma'am, one of the engines is showing a failure, so for safety reasons, we will be making an emergency landing at the nearest airport." The woman tried to stay calm, but that didn't help Nivri stay calm.

"What?" Nivri almost barked, starting to shiver.

Avinash heard the distant announcement but had ignored it. When he heard a fearful cry, the sleep shook away from him. He opened his eyes to find Nivri shivering in her seat.

"Nivri, what's wrong." Avinash put his arm around her.

"I... I don't believe this. The plane... they are doing an emergency landing." Her voice was a whisper.

"Nivri, we will be fine... it's an emergency landing, not a crash-landing." He attempted to comfort her by running his hand up and down her back.

"I don't want to die like this. No one knows I am on this plane... they will be worried sick," she whimpered.

"Nivri, look at me." His words were a command, but his voice was soft. He cupped her face when she looked up at him. "The plane is stable, and it looks like they are descending. Everything will be okay."

"This is what they said when our plane crash-landed..." He didn't let her finish.

"Nivri, I got you. Do you want me to hold you like how I held you on the other plane?"

"Yes." It was a plea.

Nivri and Avinash were in the business class, and the separation between their seats was not something he could remove. He moved as close as he could to her to hold her to him, but her breathing was still ragged.

"Hold me close to you, please." Her voice wavered.

"I can't... the seat is too..." His words trailed off when she pulled away to unclick her seat belt. He watched in amazement as she stood up to sit in his lap, her arms circling his neck.

"Nivri, what are you doing?" His breath was warm in her ear.

"I... just don't hug random men... but... I'm too..." She buried her face into his neck making him shudder. The beast in his pants came alive at the most inappropriate moment.

"Nivri, you can't sit on my lap when we are landing."

"Yes, I can... put your seat belt around me." Her voice was muffled against his neck, and he felt moisture from her eyes on his skin.

"We will be okay... please don't cry." Avinash patted her back as she continued to tremble with fear.

"I don't want anything to happen to us. I was looking forward to going on a date with you." Her confession made him smile.

"I will definitely take you on that date and—" His words got stuck in his throat when they felt the plane dip to one side in a strong jerking motion.

Nivri let out a cry against the crook of his neck, and he held her closer to him. He showed her the seat belt that was around both of them when one of the air hostesses gestured for Nivri to sit in her seat. The woman looked terrified herself to press further to make Nivri sit in her seat and strap on her seat belt.

"This is bad... I never thought this would happen to me... not when I'm all alone." Nivri continued to wail.

"Hey, I'm here with you. I may not be family, but I'm here with you."

"I'm never giving anyone any surprises. If the flight crashes, I will be one of those unidentified bodies."

"Nivri, calm down."

Nivri suddenly pulled back to look at him, her eyes puffy and red with tears. "I think you are super-hot. I've never been on a date with someone as good looking as you."

He laughed looking at her. "Why are you telling me all that now?"

"Just in case this flight..." Her words were lost in a gasp as the flight made another sudden movement this time associated with a loud noise from the outside.

"I don't want to die like this, Avinash," Nivri cried, and the tears made something deep inside him hurt.

"Please don't cry. These planes will land safely even if all engines fail... don't worry." Avinash cupped her face wiping the tears off her cheeks with his thumbs.

"Why didn't I meet you sooner?"

"I have to tell..." His words were lost when she crashed her lips to his.

Avinash blinked for a brief second before pulling her to him, his lips opening up to take her breath away. She moaned against his lips as he dipped his tongue into her warm mouth, exploring every corner. He was getting lost in the sweet moment when she pulled back making his eyes flutter open.

"I'm sorry, I shouldn't have..." she started to say, but he swallowed her words.

"I'm not sorry you kissed me," he mumbled.

Nivri smiled against his lips enjoying the devouring kiss as his lips worshiped hers. She gripped his thick, dark hair and felt his hold tighten around her waist.

"While we are confessing, I find you super-hot and was very happy when you told me you were single."

"Me, too," she said as he sucked her lower lip between his teeth, tugging it hard before letting it go.

"Will you go on a date with me before you go back to New York if we survive the crash?" He chuckled, pulling back to look up at her.

"Yes," she rasped, and the plane started to shake as the wheels hit the tarmac.

"I guess you are going out with me before you go back to New York." Avinash pointed outside the window and grinned, making her blush.

Chapter 6

"What? We crash landed in Hyderabad of all places?" Nivri got up from his lap to sit in her seat.

"Emergency landing... not crash-landing. Very different."

"How is that possible?" She looked out of the window still unable to believe she landed in her hometown.

"I can take you home." He smiled.

"I don't want to go home. My mom and dad are traveling, and that's why I am going to my grandma's village."

"I don't think you will be able to go to Bangalore tonight... not on this plane for sure." Avinash stood up, reaching for their bags and followed her out of the plane.

"I need to go to Bangalore. When will the plane be ready?" Nivri asked one of the flight attendants.

"Sorry, ma'am, we are not sure if we will be able to accommodate all the passengers on other planes. We will make sure you have hotel accommodations."

"I don't need hotel accommodations... I need a way to get to Bangalore."

"You will need to check with our ground staff, ma'am." The polite attendant gestured her to keep walking, and Avinash followed her debating if he should go with her to Bangalore or meet her when she is in Hyderabad.

Avinash considered himself to be extremely pragmatic, but every decision he made around Nivri was completely irrational, and he had no reason.

"Avinash, let's go talk to that man. You need to be in Bangalore for your meeting, right?" Nivri marched toward a man in an airline uniform.

Twenty minutes of going in circles about Nivri wanting to be on a flight to Bangalore and the airline crew telling her the earliest flight was the following afternoon, pissed her off.

"You totally ruined my grandma's surprise." Nivri tried every emotional drama in the book, but the airline crew stuck to their guns and told her they had no clearance to take off any earlier than tomorrow.

Nivri glared at the supervisor who told her she had to take care of her own transportation before walking to the baggage claim to take her bags. "I will not let anything stop me from going to my grandma's village tonight."

"Nivri, what's the hurry? Stay back in Hyderabad for one day, and you can go tomorrow."

She turned to look at Avinash her eyes spitting fire. "Hey, I told you I'll go on a date... not tonight. I need to go."

Avinash circled his fingers around her wrist. "I'm in no hurry to take you out on a date, but do you hear yourself? You just had two panic attacks within the last twenty-four hours being on a plane, and you want to get on another one?"

Nivri took a deep breath. "I need to go... I'll figure it out."

"Nivri, what are you—"

"I'll take a cab... my grandma's village is four hours from Bangalore and seven hours from Hyderabad. I'm sure I can reach my grandma's village before midnight if I start now." He saw the excitement in her eyes.

"It's not safe."

"Go with me then. You can make it to your meeting with a lot of time to spare. We will split the cost."

Avinash shook his head. "You won't get a cab outside the airport that will drive you seven hours... not the city cabs."

"You are right, but I don't want to wait or get on another plane even if it is tomorrow." Nivri sat on a bench looking dejected.

Avinash thought for a few moments before speaking. "I have an idea, I will have someone bring me my car, and I will drive to Bangalore for my meeting."

"What? Oh my God. That is a wonderful idea... I'll drive halfway." She squealed in happiness.

"Okay... give me a few minutes." Avinash spent a few minutes on the phone and arranged for someone to bring his SUV to the airport.

Almost thirty minutes later, they stepped out of the Hyderabad airport.

"I missed you, Hyderabad. I'll be back soon." Nivri took in the warm, humid air as she got into the passenger seat. The man who drove the SUV to the airport handed the keys to Avinash after helping load the bags into the vehicle.

"Are we there yet?" Nivri asked, laughing, as soon as Avinash slid into the driver's seat.

"ETA is about midnight right now."

"C'mon, Avinash, put this five hundred horsepower baby to work." She laughed.

"Yes, ma'am."

"Thank you and don't call me ma'am. I don't like that..."

"Should I call you, my lady?" he teased.

"I'm not your lady so, no," she retorted.

"If I had to call you something right now, I would say you are one bullhead."

"No... don't you ever call me that. I hate that word...never ever, Avinash." Her voice was gruff with anger.

"I got it. I just meant..."

"I know I am adamant at times but not a bullhead. I know what I am doing and why I need to do it."

"Point taken. If I'm not mistaken, there seems to be some history to why you don't like that word."

"Yes. Bunny, that moron, used to call me a bullhead, and every time he did, I wanted to punch him so hard and knock out his bunny teeth." Nivri gritted her teeth.

"Wow, easy. Who is this guy? An ex-boyfriend?"

Nivri made gagging noises. "That guy is my arch enemy. He made my childhood traumatic. I was so happy when he left India for his undergrad."

"You went to school with this guy?"

"Yeah, for a bit... can't stand talking about him. Let's talk about something else." Nivri shook her shoulders like she wanted to dust off any thoughts about the guy.

Chapter 7

Four hours into the drive, the traffic on the highway came to a standstill.

"This is unbelievable... isn't there another route?" Nivri looked up and down the highway at the vehicles that were stopped.

"Unfortunately, no. A canal is overflowing, and we need to wait until the water level goes down."

"Why is this happening to me?" Nivri hid her face in her palms.

"Hey, I'm right here... happening to me, too."

"No, you don't get it... the flight... now this..." she sounded dejected.

"Nivri, just take a nap so that you can drive later."

She nodded and slipped into the back seat and put her head down to sleep.

Hours passed, and she lay in the back seat, distant honking playing in her ear and the jerking movement that was assurance she was getting closer to her grandmother's village. She slowly opened her eyes in the darkness, her gaze falling on the man behind the wheel. He had been driving for hours, and she didn't know how to thank him for everything he had done for her. It was not like her to trust anyone from their first meeting, but something about the way he held her, the compassion he showed toward her—it felt like she had known him for a long time.

Nivri continued to look at him. His eyes were on the road, soft music was playing in the background, and moments later, she realized the sound of the rain was slashing against the windows. She looked at the windshield and realized it was raining heavily. She sat up in the back seat, rubbing her eyes.

"Good morning." Avinash chuckled looking at her in the rearview mirror.

Nivri scrunched her nose before slipping between the seats to sit in the passenger seat next to him. "How much longer?"

"A few more hours. It's just taking longer because of the rain," Avinash said, not taking his eyes off the road.

"I'm hungry," she whined.

"We should be coming up on a small town in about an hour, and they might have some restaurant options."

"I'd like some French food, please." She laughed.

"After I've seen you eat at the airport, I doubt if you've ever stepped into a French restaurant."

"You guessed it right... I canceled a date with a guy once because he had suggested a French restaurant."

"I promise not to take you to a French restaurant." He chuckled.

"I'll go wherever you want to take me."

"When will you..." A beeping noise interrupted him, and he looked at the blinking light on the dashboard.

"What's going on?" Nivri asked when he cursed and pulled the vehicle over to the side of the road. The highway they were on was not well lit, and the only light was from the SUV and the passing vehicles.

"Our night might have just gotten a lot more interesting," Avinash growled getting out of the vehicle and stepped into the rain.

"Avinash, it's raining hard, get back in," Nivri called out rolling her side of the window down as he started walking around the vehicle.

Avinash came back to sit in the driver's seat, his hair and clothes dripping wet. He ran his fingers through his damp hair and looked at her. "We have a flat tire, and I'll need to change it."

"No, you will not, not when it is raining like this," she said reaching for her purse to pull out paper towels and handed them to him.

"The rain is not going to stop anytime soon."

"I can help if you tell me what to do exactly." She smiled.

"No... I can do it..." He stopped talking but was looking out into the darkness.

Without another word, he started driving again, slowly on the side of the highway. He turned off on a mud road a few minutes later, and it was after that she saw a light in the distance.

"Is that a house?"

"I am hoping it is somewhere I can get help to change the tire." He kept his eyes on the road as the vehicle bobbed on the uneven road.

"I told you I could help you."

"It's raining, Nivri. You can't show up at your grandma's house soaking wet." He laughed.

Nivri smiled to herself looking at him as he turned the vehicle into the first house out of the three houses that were built right next to each other. Avinash stopped the vehicle under what looked like a carport and got out of the vehicle.

An elderly man stepped into the covered patio in front of the house, and Nivri saw the men shake hands and talk. From what Avinash was pointing to, she guessed he was asking the older man if he could get help changing the tire. Nivri watched as the older man handed Avinash a box that seemed to be a toolkit.

Moments passed, and the men kept talking, and Nivri got impatient. She opened the door and stepped out just when an elderly woman came out of the house. Avinash was smiling and shaking his head like he was having a tough time saying no to what the elderly couple was suggesting.

Nivri walked out to stand next to Avinash, smiling at the older couple.

"Thank you for the offer, but we will get going as soon as I change the tire." Avinash turned and smiled when their eyes met.

"Nivri, meet Mr. and Mrs. Challa."

Nivri smiled at them and greeted the older couple.

"Nivri, you should use the restroom while I change the tire," Avinash suggested.

"Yes, I would like that." Nivri smiled and followed the older woman when she gestured her to go with her.

"Would you and your husband like some coffee?" the older woman asked, and Nivri coughed out a choke. The woman continued talking, ignoring Nivri as she shook her head to correct the woman. "Did you guys get married recently? You make such a beautiful couple."

Nivri smiled stepping into the bathroom and decided not to correct the woman. She didn't need a disapproving look from an elderly woman when she found out Nivri was traveling with a complete stranger.

Avinash felt closer to her heart and soul… not a stranger.

Chapter 9

"It is not safe to drive through the forest roads, too many highway robberies happened recently," Nivri heard the older man say as she walked toward the patio. The rain was coming down hard, and she heard the wind howling outside the window.

"We only have a couple of hours to go. Nivri wants to see her grandma today," Avinash said, turning to look at Nivri as she joined them.

The elder woman touched Nivri's hand. "Your grandma would want you and your husband to be safe. Stay with us tonight and leave tomorrow morning."

Nivri looked at Avinash, and his eyes widened, but he didn't correct the woman. "Mrs. Challa, it's too much trouble for you. Thank you for your kindness."

The older woman was not ready to let go. "I will not take no for an answer. You are like our children. We cannot let you go into harm's way, knowingly."

Nivri was suddenly longing to sleep on steady ground. The idea of sleeping without worrying about planes crashing and roads being blocked suddenly started to sound appealing.

"Your wife looks so tired. She needs to eat and sleep," the older woman insisted making Nivri think of her grandma.

"Avinash... your meeting tomorrow..." she started to say and stopped when she saw something spark in his eyes.

"Don't worry about my meeting. Do you want to rest and show up at your grandma's place refreshed?" Avinash smiled.

"Yes... you are tired from all the driving, too." Nivri scrunched her nose, and the elderly couple nodded in agreement.

"Why don't you go change, child?" the woman said, and her eyes fell to Nivri's neck. The woman leaned closer and whispered, "I know it is not fashionable to wear your wedding necklace on a daily basis, but you should wear it, especially because you will be visiting your grandma."

Nivri grinned. "Yes, I have it in my purse. I put it away for travel."

"It is safe to wear here. Go change, and I will have food ready for you both." The older woman gestured to a young man who was waiting by Avinash's SUV to bring the bags inside.

"I just need my small bag," she said looking at Avinash, trying to gauge his reaction to everything that the older couple said.

"I'll bring it," Avinash said and turned away from her.

Nivri followed the older woman into the house and up the stairs to one of the bedrooms. "All our children live in the city, so now we have so much space."

Nivri looked around the large bedroom and was glad to see a small sofa to one side by the window. "You have a beautiful home. Thank you for hosting us for the night."

The elderly woman smiled. "You are welcome, child. The bathroom is through that door. Please take your time to take a bath. I will get the dinner set out."

"Mrs. Challa, please don't go to too much trouble. I am not hungry." Nivri smiled.

"You look like you haven't eaten in days. Come down when you are ready to eat." The elderly woman left before Nivri could object again.

Nivri walked over to the window and looked outside. The window overlooked the area where a couple of cars, a jeep, and a tractor were parked. She saw the area light up and then saw Avinash park his SUV. She watched from the bedroom window at the upper level as he turned on the light on the inside of the vehicle to reach for her bag on the back seat that she had asked for their overnight stay.

She smiled, her heart filled with gratitude for the man who had helped her like no one ever has before. Her smile froze when his hand went to the scarf that was lying on the back seat, his fingers gently grazing over the thin material before he fisted his fingers in the fabric. She watched without blinking her eyes as he sat back in the driver's seat looking at the scarf as if there was something on it.

Just as Nivri wondered if there was a stain on the scarf that caught his attention, he took the fabric to his face. She saw him take a slow, deep breath from her scarf through the rain and the dim light on the inside of the vehicle. Her hands gripped the metal grill on the window as her stomach knotted up.

He held the scarf to his face for a few moments before turning to put it inside her bag. He picked up her backpack, slipped his on his hand, and went up to the roof of the vehicle to turn off the light. As if he sensed her presence, he looked up at the window and right at her.

Nivri's breath hitched, and her heart started to race when he smiled at her. She managed to wave at him while her knees felt weak. Avinash turned off the light inside the vehicle and rushed out to avoid getting wetter. She turned away from the window, pressing her back into the wall next to it. She stood still and waited for him.

Avinash's slightest sounds from every movement of his as he walked up the stairs to the bedroom boomed in her head. She shut her eyes to calm her nerves as the pulse at her temple throbbed in anticipation.

"Hey, you okay?" His voice was soft, and her eyes flew open.

She pressed her lips together and nodded.

"I don't know why they assumed we were married but..."

She laughed in an attempt to fight what seemed to be some tension looming over them. "I have no idea, and I was worried she would kick us out if I told her I never met you before... thirty-six hours ago."

Avinash chuckled walking toward her and stopped a foot away placing both the bags in his hands on the floor.

"I'm sorry I wasn't able to take you to your destination tonight."

"Avinash, please don't apologize. You have no idea how grateful I am to be traveling with you. I was not thinking straight at the airport, and I..."

Nivri swallowed her words when he stepped closer into her personal space, flattening his palms on the wall, on either side of her. "Don't be grateful for anything. It is my pleasure to travel with you."

She smiled looking up into his eyes that got darker by the second with a raw spark in them.

"I need to shower," she said, breaking their gaze, and he immediately pushed off the wall and stepped away from her.

"I'll shower downstairs." He turned away picking up his backpack and stopped when she called out to him.

Nivri walked close to him. "I... I need to borrow your chain."

"What?"

She pointed to the thick gold chain that hung around his neck, most of it hidden under his shirt. "I need to wear something around my neck. I don't have anything, and elderly people are very traditional, especially—"

Avinash let out a chuckle and pulled off the gold chain and handed it to her. It was a long, thick chain with a pendant that looked like the character 'A.'

She slipped it over her head and around her neck. It hit her mid-chest. "Thank you, I'll give it back to you tomorrow."

Avinash looked at her for a long moment, his eyes scanning her face, then falling to look at his chain on her chest and smiled mischievously before leaving her alone.

Chapter 10

Nivri ran her fingers through her damp curls to tame the wild strands. She stood in front of the mirror looking at herself grinning from ear to ear like a fool. She had no idea what made her so happy, but she couldn't help smiling at her reflection. She adjusted the thick cotton tunic she put on after her shower and used her eyeliner to put a black dot on her forehead. She gave herself one final perusal adjusting Avinash's chain around her neck before heading downstairs for dinner.

She went down the stairs, her every step soft as she focused on Avinash's voice. He seemed to be in a conversation with Mr. Challa about the state politics.

"There you are. Avinash didn't want to start eating without you," the elderly woman said, and it almost sounded like a tease.

"Oh..."

"Not sure when you two ate last during your long journey," the elderly woman asked, and it was at that point she realized Avinash only had a coffee at the New Delhi airport.

Nivri turned to look at Avinash and blurted. "Avinash, you should eat... you haven't eaten anything all day."

The way he smiled at her made her stomach flutter, and she muttered an apology for interrupting the conversation he was having with Mr. Challa.

Nivri ate quietly listening to Avinash converse with ease with the older couple. She wondered if that is how he would interact with her grandma.

Why was she thinking about his interaction with her grandma? Stop it, Nivri!

"Nivri..." His voice seemed distant, and she looked up from her plate in Avinash's direction. "You are not eating."

She smiled at everyone at the table and took a bite of the steaming hot food. "Tastes really good, Mrs. Challa."

"You should eat well, Nivri. You need to be strong enough to bear all your future children," the elderly woman said, and Nivri choked on the sip of water she had taken just at that moment. She managed to nod when Avinash asked if she was okay. She was grateful the conversations shifted to politics from talking about how a group of dacoits was stopping private cars and looting people for the rest of the meal. A shiver ran through her spine when she realized she was going to travel in a taxi all by herself. She looked at Avinash and thanked her stars for him being with her.

Shortly after dinner, Nivri stood up from the patio where they were sitting watching the rain come down. She had a heavy meal and was super sleepy. "Good night, Mr. and Mrs. Challa."

"Avinash, you should go sleep, too. Mr. Challa can talk politics all night if you are willing to listen." The elderly woman laughed.

Nivri walked away from the group, her legs feeling tired, her eyes droopy as she climbed the stairs, one step at a time, her fingers gripping the wooden railing for support. She stopped and turned to look when she heard him behind her, and the turning motion made her lose her footing.

Suddenly, she was falling, and her grip tightened on the railing, but she felt her fingers slip off of the support bar, and she let out a squeal and closed her eyes bracing for the impact.

She fell back but did not hit anything, and then she felt his hands pushing her back into a standing position as he came to stand behind her, on a lower step, his eyes level with hers as she stood a step higher.

"Nivri, what's wrong?" His tone held concern, and his hands caressed her waist.

She looked into his eyes, a sudden urge to hug him surfaced, and she threw her arms around him sobbing for reasons she could not explain.

He held her to him, hushing her gently, whispering in her ear. "I'm right here."

"Avi...Avinash, I don't know what I would have done if you weren't with me. I was so stupid to think I could take a cab to go to my grandma's village." She sniffled and pulled back to look at him.

Avinash smiled at her, wiping the tears off her cheeks. "You should go to bed."

She nodded looking at him and turned to climb the remaining few steps with Avinash right behind her. She stopped at the door when she felt him step away.

"Where are you going?" she asked.

He smiled walking toward her, his hands in his shorts' pockets. "There are three other bedrooms on this level."

"Oh... I was actually prepared to sleep on that sofa." She smiled.

"No... sleep comfortably on the bed, and I will be in the room next door. Good night," he said and leaned forward, his eyes locked with hers as he kissed her cheek.

Nivri felt her heart flutter and her stomach clench as he started to pull back. A sudden urge to clash her lips with his was overwhelming. She fisted her fingers on his shirt, not letting him pull away and looked up into his eyes.

"Avinash... I want..."

He swallowed her words into a hungry kiss. His lips crashed into hers, and she welcomed the pressure as it relieved what was building up inside her. She gasped into his mouth when he pulled her close to him, his hands pressing into the small of her back. He pushed into her making her walk backward into the bedroom as his tongue explored her warm mouth.

Nivri wrapped her arms around him and felt weightless as he pulled her to him, her feet lifting off the ground. She kissed him back matching the urgency in the devouring moment and gasped for air when he let go of her lips and trailed them down the column of her neck, nibbling and suckling on her skin, making her moan.

"Nivri... you keep making that sound, and I won't be able to stop," he groaned deep inside.

Nivri pressed her fingers deeper into his hair, pressing her face further into her neck, in response to what he was doing to her. "Don't stop..."

Avinash reached out to shut the door, his mouth never leaving hers. "You smell so good."

Nivri dug her fingernails into his skin sending shudders through him. "Sleep with me, here."

He let go of her lips leaving butterfly kisses along her jawline. "Do you think that's a good idea?"

"Yes, I'm scared. Don't leave me alone." It was a plea.

"Baby, why are you scared?" He pulled back to look at her.

"What if I had taken the taxi? Those highway robbers..."

He didn't let her finish. "I would have never let you take that taxi... no way." He walked her backward to the bed, and when the back of her knees hit the bed, she collapsed, pulling his weight on to her, laughing.

"You need to rest tonight, good night." He kissed her on her forehead and rolled to the other side of the bed.

"Okay, sleep in this room... I'll sleep on the sofa if you want the bed." She smiled, sitting up.

He looked at her for a long moment and smiled, teasingly. "Okay, I'll sleep here if you stay on your side."

"Fine, I will." She laughed shaking her head.

Chapter 11

Shortly after, Nivri brushed her teeth and stepped out of the bathroom after changing into a nightshirt, ready to settle in for the night. She almost laughed out loud when she saw how Avinash was passed out on the sofa, his laptop still on his lap, his head fallen back in the backrest of the small sofa.

She tiptoed to him and stood a foot from him, her eyes riveted on his handsome face. "Avinash." When he didn't move, she picked up the laptop off his lap and placed it on the nightstand next to the bed. She turned to look at him and debated whether to wake him up or not. He looked extremely uncomfortable, and she wanted him to sleep well. She sat on the sofa next to him and made the sofa move enough for him to wake up, but he didn't move.

Nivri smiled looking at his face, his rugged features relaxed as he slept, a slight smile on his face as if he were dreaming about something that made him happy. She leaned closer to him, and she told herself she wanted to whisper his name, so she didn't startle him when he woke up. She went up on her knees, her knee-caps pushing down on the sofa as she got closer to his ear. She rested one hand on the backrest behind him and was inches from his face when his eyes flew open.

She let out a gasp, and before she could say anything, she was crashing onto him, his lips conquering hers. He wrapped his arms around her. "Oh, I was dreaming about you."

His words made her squirm in his arms as his hands roamed her body.

"I was trying to wake you up," she murmured against his lips.

"Why?" His hand moved from her back to cup her breast, possessively.

"Maybe I wanted to be kissed like this." She smiled against his lips.

"And?"

"Touch me like this." She placed her hand over his that caressed her breast.

"And?"

"I don't know..."

"Has anyone touched you before?"

"Not like this... no one," she confessed.

"Are you sure you want this?" He let her breast go and ran the back of his hand over her pulsating folds making her realize that his touch would take the dull ache away.

"I want you." Her voice held a command.

"You'll have to wait until I take you out on that date," he groaned, nibbling on her lower lip.

"Don't tease me like that," she moaned as his lips trailed lower, his hand fumbling with the buttons on her nightshirt. She reached for the hem of his t-shirt and pulled back to pull it over his head and toss it on the floor.

His hands cupped her face bringing her lips to press against his and mold her body to his. She ran her hands over his arms enjoying the feel of rock-hard muscles on his arms.

"You are so hard," she mumbled, digging her fingers into his biceps.

"You think?" He pulled back smiling to take her hand to his crotch.

She gasped when she felt his hardness, the symbol of his need for her, and she swore she felt the throbbing through the thin material of his shorts.

She smiled at him, mischievously. "You are so hard."

Avinash let out a growl as he pulled her onto his lap on the sofa, her knees deep into the cushion on his sides, her body arched and her throbbing clit was rubbing against his steely shaft. She shuddered in response to the wave of pleasure that rippled through her when she felt him soothe the impending pressure through the thin fabric of his shorts.

Nivri moaned when she felt something building inside her, something very foreign to her. She gripped his hair with one hand and threw her head back and gave in to her body's need to rub her throbbing core against his hardness. She let out a low squeal when he pushed aside the fabric of her nightshirt to expose her breast before his large hand cupped it.

"Beautiful," he mumbled as he took his lips to the valley between her breasts, slowly running the tip of his tongue along the curve of her breast to finally take her pebbled nipple into his warm mouth. She took in a deep breath, biting down on her lip when she felt the eruption from inside, a surge of uncontrollable sensations that swept through her body making her shudder.

"Avinash," she rasped his name, and at that moment, he bit down on the softness of her breast, and that pushed her over the edge, making her collapse onto his shoulder, her breathing ragged.

She felt the throbbing, the tingling, and most of all, the sweet pain from the spot where she had felt his teeth sink into her skin. She hugged him as she gathered herself, and he ran his hands over her back, molding her to him like he didn't want to let her go.

Nivri wanted to stay in his arms. She didn't want to move, but she pulled back when she felt him gather her closer and got up with her, her legs wrapping around him. He placed her on the bed and lay down next to her, looking at her, silently.

"Why are you looking at me like that?"

"Because you are beautiful." He reached closer to plant a kiss on her forehead making her blush.

"I... I..." She attempted to speak, not knowing what to say.

"I want you, Nivri... more than you want me, but I don't want this to be a rushed affair. I want us to know each other well, and I want to do this right." He ran his fingers through her messy curls.

She smiled at him appreciating his candor. "I like you."

"I like you, too, and I want you to sleep now."

"I will." She scooted closer to him wrapping his arm around her with her cheek to his bare chest.

"Sleep tight, sweetness. I promise you a lot of sleepless nights in the future," he whispered, his breath warm in her ear, and she smiled. She shut her eyes letting the drumming in his heart be her lullaby.

Chapter 11

Nivri rolled in bed missing the warmth that caressed her through the night. She was very aware of his arm around her all night, and she wasn't sure where he was at that moment. She lay in bed, and she got her answer moments later. His voice drifted in through the open window with the cool morning breeze. She could still remember the way he kissed, touched, and made her hit peaks like never before.

She smiled rolling out of bed to look out of the window. He was by his SUV changing the punctured tire as he conversed with Mr. Challa. She looked at how genuinely and with so much ease he conversed, and a thought passed through her mind.

Would he have been like this if her grandpa were around? She remembered the conversation she had with her grandpa about a prince charming. Her grandpa was sure to tell her a prince charming was not someone who would ride a horse and sweep her off her feet, but someone who was smart, compassionate, would treat her like a queen, and be respectful to elders.

She smiled to herself and headed into the bathroom to shower and be on their way to her grandma's village.

Almost an hour later, she hugged Mrs. Challa for her generosity and hospitality. "Thank you… you are just like my grandma."

"Bless you, my child." The older woman smiled and handed her a bag of snacks.

Avinash loaded the bags into the SUV, and they left the older couple's home, Nivri smiling ear to ear as they drove closer to her grandma's village.

"I'm so full. I could use a nap right about now," Avinash said.

"I can drive," Nivri offered.

"Be my beautiful navigator." He laughed reaching for chewing gum from the center console between the seats.

"Is that gum?" she asked, scrunching her nose.

"Yeah…"

"Please throw it away. I… I hate that smell… I cannot… I'll give you my mints." She looked disgusted.

"Nivri, its regular gum… why are you…"

"I can't. I won't ever kiss you if you chew gum," she blurted handing him her mints.

Avinash laughed. "Easy… what's going on?"

"You don't what to know…" She turned away from him looking out of the window.

He reached out to pat her on her knee. "Nivri, I want to know everything about you."

"I don't want to talk about it."

"Okay... you don't need to tell me if you are not comfortable with..."

"I don't want to talk about that idiot, Bunny. I hate him," she growled, and Avinash went silent waiting for her to continue.

"This guy made my childhood hell, and he was the reason I had to shave my head when I was in ninth grade... ninth grade... can you imagine?" Her voice was a roar.

"What happened?" His voice was suddenly low.

"Bunny was chewing gum, a lot of it. It had to be the entire pack, and I don't even remember why, but I tackled him, and that idiot spit all the chewing gum from his mouth, and it got stuck in my hair, like all over my curly hair.... eeew." She shivered outwardly.

"Oh..."

"And because of how curly my hair is, the more I tried to pull it out, the messier it got. I had to sleep with that gum in my hair all night before the hair salon lady said it was better to shave my head. Aaargh, it was so bad. I was the talk of the school, and I could smell the chewing gum for months... I hate it."

"I'm sorry." His voice was low, and he squeezed her knee.

"I hated that guy. I never ever want to see him, ever."

"Okay, I won't chew gum. I want you to kiss me." He winked.

She smiled. "When will I see you?"

"Spend some time with your grandma. I'll attend my meeting today and call you tomorrow."

"Okay." She blushed.

Two hours and exciting conversations later, Nivri squealed when she saw the sign for her grandma's village. She talked about her memories in the village as they drove on the muddy and bumpy road.

"That's the house... you see how beautiful it is... and look, that treehouse... my grandpa built it for me. I missed this place so much." Nivri fought back happy tears.

"You look so happy," he said, smiling at her.

"You gave me this happiness. I would have missed this if I had come at night. Thank you!"

Avinash smiled and followed her directions toward the huge mansion surrounded by greenery and stopped right outside the main entrance. The guard at the gate saw Nivri and smiled affectionately.

"Nivri, madam. What are you doing here?" The young man looked shocked.

She hushed him. "It's a surprise to Grandma..."

"I'll take the bags in," the young man said unloading her bags and walking toward the house.

"Dhora, don't let her see my bags," Nivri called out after the young man and turned to look at Avinash who was looking at her quietly. "Let's go. I want you to meet my grandma."

He reached out, his hand cupping her cheek. "You go… I'll meet her next time I come here."

"No… now," she whined.

"I need to go. I'll see you tomorrow." His voice was soft.

"I'll miss you," she said and threw her arms around him.

Avinash pulled back to kiss her on her forehead. "I'll see you soon. I have to go now."

"Call me," she called out as he drove away smiling like a fool.

"Nivri?" She heard her grandma call her, and she turned smiling at her grandma.

"Surprise! I'm here to celebrate Diwali with you!" Nivri laughed.

Chapter 12

Later that day, she was taking a walk with her grandma in the fields behind the house.

"You traveled by yourself," her grandma said for almost the tenth time, almost surprised.

"I tried... it's a good thing I had a friend."

"I still cannot believe you didn't invite your friend inside," her grandma grumbled.

"It's okay, Nani. He said he had a meeting." Nivri felt her cheeks heat up just at the thought of Avinash. She had a tough time not calling him all day and kept wondering what he was doing. Secretly, she had hoped for him to call her and was waiting for her phone to ring.

"Nivri... are you even listening to what I am saying?" her grandma interrupted her thoughts.

"What? Yeah, I am." She had no clue what her grandma said.

"So, you are okay to meet him?" The elderly woman went on.

"Meet who?" Nivri was paying attention.

"Who were you thinking about?" her grandma teased.

"Stop, Nani. He is just a guy I met on the plane."

"And you are still thinking about him?"

"Well, he helped me a lot. I talked to him for hours... told him about Grandpa. You know, I think Grandpa would have liked him." Nivri's eyes sparkled.

Her grandmother sat on the bench looking up at her. "Is this 'friend' of yours worth mentioning to your dad?"

"What? Why? Oh gosh... please. Will you guys stop with the matchmaking. I am not ready for any of it."

"Nivri, you know your father is going to bring it up, and I know he wants you to meet Kishore."

"He can bring it up all he wants, I'm not getting married yet. Wait... who the heck is Kishore?"

"You know Kishore... Deepa aunty and Gopal uncle's son. You guys were friends when you were young." Her grandma smiled.

Nivri's grit her teeth at the mention of the name. "You mean Bunny? That moron and I were never friends, I hated him... I would never..."

Her grandmother didn't let her finish. "Nivri, calm down."

"Nani, you have no idea how much I... He was the one who put gum in my hair in ninth grade... remember?"

Her grandma laughed, annoying Nivri. "That was by mistake."

"He put salt in my wine," Nivri barked.

Her grandma laughed. "*Your* wine? You were thirteen, and you stole your mother's drink."

"Whatever, I don't want to talk about him."

"Okay, just tell your dad you don't want to meet Kishore when he talks to you about him."

"I will, and thank you for the heads up." She hugged her grandma.

"Did you call your dad?"

Nivri laughed. "Yes, I called him from your phone and left Mom and Dad a message on the answering machine at the hotel. I am sure that will confuse him like crazy."

Her grandma laughed with her. "I am sure we will get a call very soon."

Nivri and her grandma had barely stepped into the house when the phone started to ring. Nivri laughed and answered the call. "Hello?"

"Nivri?"

"Hi, Daddy!"

"Sweetheart... where are you?" Her dad sounded suspicious, and she started laughing. "Where are you?" he asked again, and her grandma also started to laugh.

"I'm in India with Nani, Daddy."

"Nivri, are you joking?"

"Surprise! I am here to celebrate Diwali with you all in the village," Nivri said, cheerfully.

"That is wonderful, dear. I can't wait to see you. We will take the next flight out of London."

"Daddy, you will do no such thing... I want you to wrap up the conversations you are having with folks there, and you know how much Mom loves to explore London."

"Your mom wants to go back, too." Her father sounded excited.

"No... I want to spend some alone time with Nani. Please don't ruin it." She winked looking at her grandmother.

Her father laughed. "I will wrap up all my meetings in a day, and we will see you in a few days."

"That sounds good, Dad."

"I'm so happy you are there with Nani, Nivri."

"Me, too, Daddy." Nivri put an arm around her grandma.

"Nivri... Oh hang on, Mom wants to talk."

"Daddy, wait!"

"What is it, sweetie?"

"You will get an approval request to sponsor a fourteen-year-old kid named Raju from New Delhi."

"New Delhi?"

"I'll tell you later but just approve it. I have already reviewed the numbers with Mr. Hassan."

"You make me so proud, Nivri. There was a special mention of the education foundation we support at one of the meetings here in London."

"Good job, Daddy." She smiled.

"I told everyone in the room that you get full credit for the education program. It was your idea, and you deserve every bit of the success." Her father's voice was filled with pride.

"You are biased, Daddy. You know I could not have done it without you and Mr. Hassan."

"Love you, sweetheart. Talk to your mother now."

"Love you, too, Daddy."

"Baby, are you really in India?" Her mom was in disbelief.

"Yes, Ma."

"I'm so proud of you... you traveled by yourself."

Nivri smiled. "For the record, I had multiple panic attacks, but the guy sitting next to me helped."

"That's nice. Why didn't you tell us you were coming to India?"

"Because it is a surprise." She laughed.

"I know, dear, but... I don't want you to travel by yourself again. Whenever you are going back to New York, I will go with you or send Daddy."

"Ma, please... I am twenty-two years old, I think I can manage."

"No, sweetheart..."

Nivri cut her mother off. "Mom, we'll discuss this later. Enjoy the rest of your trip, and I will see you guys in a few days."

"Bye, sweetheart. I am so happy you're in India. I was so sad we were going to miss you again at Diwali."

"Love you, Ma. Hug Daddy for me." Nivri smiled and ended the call. She was happy to be with her loved ones but felt an emptiness— she was missing Avinash and wanted to see him.

Chapter 13

Nivri rolled in bed and checked the time for probably the fiftieth time that night. The time on the bedside clock showed a quarter past three in the early morning. She told herself she was jetlagged, but she knew why she could not sleep— she couldn't get Avinash out of her mind.

The chain he had let her borrow at Mr. and Mrs. Challa's home was still with her, and she picked up the A-shaped pendant off her chest and brought it to her lips. Her lips stretched into a smile at the thought of him. He was a complete stranger—she had met men who were gorgeous if not as good looking as Avinash, but no one left her sleepless.

She got out of bed and reached for her phone on the dresser and checked her messages. Nothing from Avinash. She couldn't understand why she was expecting him to be messaging her. A small voice in her head said that she needed to let him know that she still had his gold chain with her, although she wasn't ready to part with it.

Nivri: *Hey.*

She hit send and cringed realizing she had sent him a message that late at night. She knew there was desperation written all over her text. She typed fast not to make her sound so desperate.

Nivri: *I just realized I still had the chain you gave me yesterday... day before yesterday, technically.*

She stared at her phone to make sure her messages were marked as sent and almost dropped her phone when it started to ring.
It was him!
Nivri had a tough time containing her excitement. "Hey, why are you up so late?"

He laughed making her stomach flutter and something throb deep inside her. "I should be asking you the same question."

"I was... I..."

"I'm glad you messaged me." His tone softened.

"Me, too..."

"I've been in calls all day and didn't get a chance to call you. It was late by the time I was done, and I was worried I would wake you if I called."

"Avinash, I've been waiting all day to talk to you. I couldn't sleep. I kept thinking about you. Sorry if this sounds weird, but that's how I feel," she blurted and bit her tongue.

"I'm very glad to hear that, and I can't stop thinking about you either. I want to see you."

"Me, too." She let out a partial sob.

"Meet me in your treehouse in ten minutes." His voice was rushed, and she could hear him descending a flight of stairs.

"Did you say ten minutes?"

"Yes."

She let out a squeal and hung up running toward the bathroom. She knew she didn't have time to shower, but she wanted to brush her teeth, wash her face, and tame her unruly hair.

Five minutes later, she tiptoed downstairs making sure she didn't wake anyone in the household up. Her grandma had a distant relative's family living with her to take care of her, and they were the ones to cultivate the lands they owned.

The treehouse was outside the main compound of the large ancestral home, but it was not far. She could see it from the large patio in the back of the house, and the path to the treehouse was through lush gardens that her grandma cared for dearly.

Nivri walked toward the treehouse following the path lined with small solar lamps. She had initially intended to change out of her t-shirt and yoga pants into something nicer, but in her eagerness to see Avinash, she left her room and couldn't get herself to go back. She looked around the darkness looking for signs of Avinash.

"He said ten minutes not ten hours, right?" she mumbled to herself as she got closer to the treehouse. She leaned against the trunk of the large tree that held the treehouse together and looked in the direction of the road that would lead to the main house.

Nivri's heart rate sped up when she saw a vehicle's headlights, and moments later, the vehicle pulled off the main road onto the farm road headed toward her.

"Avinash." She let out a gasp and watched as the vehicle came to a stop behind another vehicle stationed at the end of the narrow side road. She saw the headlights turn off, and she looked into the darkness waiting for her eyes to adjust again.

She blinked, her eyes craving to see him, and when she saw his outline in the moonlight, the emptiness she had been feeling all day melted away. She stood rooted to her spot when her heart beat so rapidly like it wanted to leap out of her chest. She placed her palm on her heart hoping for it to settle down as he got closer to her.

"Nivri," he called out to her, softly.

"I'm here." She waved her phone with the screen illuminated.

Nivri took a few steps toward him unable to bear the wait. She stopped at the end of the raised platform that circled the tree, and when he came close enough, literally leaped into his arms.

"Baby," he growled in her ear as he wrapped his arms around her as she buried her face into his neck, her legs going around his hips.

"Avinash, I missed you."

"I missed you, too, Nivri." He pulled back to brush his lips over her making her sigh. His hand clenched in her hair as he kissed her fervently. She matched his kiss with her longing to be with him, to be kissed like he was kissing her, and she didn't care that she only knew him for a couple of days. Something told her deep inside, they were meant to meet the way they did.

Avinash pulled back to look at her in the moonlight, his hand caressing her cheek while his thumb ran over her shiny lower lip. "Just like I remembered, beautiful."

She smiled, blushing. "You saw me yesterday."

"That was too long ago..."

"I feel that way, too, and I've never felt like this before." She let go of him when he put her feet back on the raised platform before climbing it.

Avinash pulled her into his arms to kiss her cheek. "Will you give me the grand tour of the treehouse?"

"Yes, let's go. I got it cleaned earlier today." She took his hand and led him up the winding stairs into her space, ready to share it with him—only him.

"Wow, this is beautiful." Avinash let out a breath stepping into the low-ceiling treehouse. He looked out into the darkness, the outline of trees at a distance. She turned on the lamp that sat in the corner of the one-room treehouse. He sat on the bed as she opened the French doors on one side and came back to lie down on the bed and look at him.

"Welcome to my space." She smiled. He smiled back, leaning down to run his lips over hers and lowered himself to sleep next to her.

She cuddled into him, looking into his eyes as his arms wrapped around her. "I've always loved sleeping here, looking out into the night sky and the stars and…"

He swallowed her words into his mouth, his tongue caressing hers. "Good night, baby. Sleep tight."

Chapter 14

The early morning light streamed in through the partially open French doors as Nivri came out of her suspended state. She moaned feeling the comforting warmth from the man who hugged her in her sleep. It didn't take long for her to slip into a suspended state as soon as his arms wrapped around hers earlier that morning.

Nivri moaned, turning her head to look at Avinash who was still sleeping. She smiled to herself, moving slowly as she removed her hand from under his shirt. Her fingers tingled from losing contact with his warm skin. She reached for her phone and called her grandma.

"Are you in the treehouse?" her grandma asked before even Nivri said anything.

"Yes." She blushed.

"I went to your room when I woke up and knew you had slipped out in the middle of the night."

"Yes, Nani... you know how much I love it here." She stepped into the balcony of the treehouse and waved at her grandma who was enjoying her coffee in the garden.

Her grandma waved back. "I know... I will send coffee with someone."

"Nani, I need an extra-large cup of coffee... I need the caffeine." She wasn't ready to tell her grandma about Avinash, not because she would oppose her spending time with him, but because she, herself, was figuring out what was going on between them.

Nivri went back into the small room and looked at the man sleeping in her bed. It was her bed, she had not let anyone sleep there—not her parents, not her friends—only him. She walked to the door and went down the spiral stairs to meet the young boy who brought her coffee and a couple of books.

In the past, she would spend hours reading in the treehouse, and her grandma sent her books out of habit. She took the coffee and the books thanking the young man and went up the spiral stairs.

Nivri slowly opened the door and closed it ever so softly and yet, he stirred in his sleep, and his eyes fluttered open.

"Good morning," she said, placing the books and coffee flask on the floor next to the mattress.

"Good morning," he mumbled sitting up, running his fingers through his sleep sexy hair.

Nivri went down on her knees on the wooden floor, next to the mattress, her eyes level with his and leaned close to him. He reached out, pulling her off the floor and onto him, his back hitting the mattress.

Avinash's lips brushed hers ever so softly, but she felt the thrills she did every time he kissed her. She moaned enjoying his morning wood digging into her belly as he held her to him, craving for that thickness to be part of her. She was happy where they were with intimacy and was happier about the growing bond between them. Sleeping in his arms was bliss, there was no other way to explain it.

"Avinash," she rasped against his lips.

He growled in response rolling her onto her back and trailing kisses down her neck and chest. She arched her back as he pushed up her t-shirt to expose the creamy skin of her belly, kissing her belly button.

Nivri dug her fingernails into his shoulder and clenched her inner depths when he took a bite on the curve of her waist. She was lost in a pool of delectable sensations but was very aware of the moisture that surged between her folds. He worshipped her with his lips before going up to kiss her on her lips. "Now, that's how I'd like to say *good morning*."

She hugged him, enjoying the weight as she shuddered with new pleasure.

Nivri wasn't sure how long she lay in his arms, looking at the sun coming up over the trees, but she wanted to be in his arms forever.

"I want to take you out today," he whispered, running his fingers through her hair.

"Will we finally go on that date?"

He chuckled. "Yeah... I have a few things to show you. I think you will like it."

"Yeah? What I liked most was sleeping here, like this with you."

"Me, too, baby."

She tilted her head to look at him. "How did you get here so fast last night... well, this morning."

Avinash smiled, kissing the tip of her nose. "I realized I had work to do in the neighboring village, so I stayed back."

Nivri frowned and gently slapped his chest. "You were ten minutes away, and you didn't come to see me?"

"Nivri... I needed you to be sure about how you felt about me." His voice was low but intense.

"Avi..."

He didn't let her finish. "I love you, Nivri, and I cannot stop thinking about you."

She blushed. "I kept thinking to myself if what I felt was love. Now I know I love you, Avinash. I don't know how it happened... it did... it's magical."

Avinash pulled her into a slow, soft kiss that made her heart go on a rampage. She could not believe she had fallen in love, but she couldn't ask for anything more.

All she wanted was him.

Chapter 15

"Avinash, I had so much fun." Nivri laughed enjoying the cool breeze through her hair as she sat behind him on a motorbike, the sun setting behind them. The village roads were bumpy, dusty, and narrow, but none of it bothered her as she toured the area with Avinash.

Avinash had taken her to the neighboring village to show how his company had adopted the entire village changing everything for the good. Her tour started with the hospital where the equipment his company made was being used. While touring the hospital, she smiled every time she saw the name 'Nash' on the equipment, and it gave her a great sense of happiness.

The man she had fallen in love with was not only a successful businessman but one with a good heart, and it gave her a lot of pleasure knowing that his heart beat for her, just like hers did for him.

The cherry on the top for the tour was the school that Avinash took her to. It was in the middle of a rural area but running high-end equipment for students to be part of any classroom they chose to be in, from any part of the world. What she had started as an education sponsorship program with her father's help was only a step toward where Avinash was with the education programs. The moment she saw a kid from one of the surrounding villages build a robot out of Legos and showed them a demo of how the robot could move a small object from one place to another, she had tears in her eyes.

Nivri was an undeniable patriot at heart, and at that moment, she knew he was in her heart to stay, to own it for life.

"I'm glad you enjoyed the tour." He smiled.

"I liked it so much, you almost made me cry a few times." She laughed.

"Happy to hear that you are happy."

"So happy that I'll still kiss you even if you chew gum which you know how much I hate." She tightened her hold around him as they rode through narrow village roads on the motorbike.

Avinash patted her hand with his as he drove toward her grandma's village. He pulled in front of the house and waited for her to get off the bike.

"Avinash, you have to come in to meet my grandma."

He cupped her cheek with his hand. "I promise I will meet her soon, but today, I really need to go to Bangalore."

Disappointment hit her immediately. "I was hoping we could have dinner in the treehouse."

"Not tonight, love." He leaned closer to her to brush his lips over her cheek and trail them over her lips.

"What if I can't sleep?" She felt silly asking him that question, and she had never thought she would be so stupidly in love.

"I will call you. I'll talk you into sleep."

She smiled, her cheeks turning crimson. "When will I see you again?"

"In a couple of days... hopefully sooner."

"Take me with you." It was a plea.

"Nivri, you are here to spend time with your family."

She nodded, but all she wanted to do was scream and throw a fit or even beg him to take her with him. "I'll miss you... come back soon."

"You know I'll miss you, too." He smiled before putting the motorbike in gear. He gave her a long look before nodding and driving away. She stood in the dust cloud, the image of him leaving turning blurry by the second.

Nivri blinked away the tears that threatened to roll down her cheeks. She took a deep breath wondering how she was going to go back to New York with such separation anxiety for the man she had only known a few days.

She was lost in thought as she walked past the wide entrance of the house and almost jumped when she heard an overly familiar male voice call out to her. She turned and looked straight into the loving eyes of her father.

"Daddy!" she squealed and ran into his open arms.

"I missed you, Daddy," she sobbed holding him. She was seeing him for the first time since he had minor heart surgery.

Her father kissed the top of her head. "I know, sweetheart. Your mother and I could not be in London for one more second knowing you were in India."

"I'm so glad you came. Where's Mom?"

"Your mother and grandma are in the garden enjoying their tea. Let's go join them."

"Daddy, did you approve the education sponsor funds?"

"Yes, I did. First thing I did as soon as I landed in India."

"Good. I just visited a neighboring village that has gone through some amazing transformation. I think we should do something like that, too... pick a village and sponsor for everything they need to be self-sustainable, then move on to another village... like building a way for the villages to help each other."

"That's a wonderful idea, dear."

"I know someone who has worked on such rural development projects, and I can get help." She was excited as they stepped into the garden.

"Nivri, it makes me very proud to hear you have such aspirations, but I don't know how I feel about you pursuing this work."

She stopped walking and stood rooted in her spot. "What do you mean, Daddy?"

Her father turned to look at her. "I want you to enjoy your life, sweetheart. You don't need this hardship."

"Dad, don't be ridiculous. You were the one who encouraged me every step of the way. You are a role model of hard work, and you want me to stay away from hardship?"

Her father shook his head. "I've worked hard so that you don't have to do it, ever. If everything were up to me, you would be with your mother and me and not be in New York all by yourself."

"Daddy, I miss you guys, too, but it's for my education."

"I never wanted you to go to New York for college. I was hoping you would have a fun and relaxed life."

Nivri looked at her father like he was a stranger. "Dad, I can't believe you said that. You know why I got on that plane. I see myself in your job... I want your job someday."

Her father shook his head. "I don't want you to have to do my job, not that you are not capable, but I'd rather you have your mother's job of a wife and mother."

"Don't be ridiculous, Daddy."

"Call me ridiculous, selfish, whatever you want to call me. I don't want you to go through the hardship that I went through... never. You are my princess, and I will find you a prince who will treat you like a queen." Her father was getting emotional, and she could sense the conversation was going somewhere where she didn't want it to go.

"That's not up to you, Daddy. If you don't want me to be in your job, I will work on getting a similar job or start my own company."

Her father stepped closer to her. "Nivri, in all of your twenty-two years, have I ever said no to anything you wanted?"

Nivri slowly shook her head.

"I wanted to stop you from getting on that plane to New York knowing how much it would cause pain to you... but I didn't want to say no."

"Daddy, I can't be scared of flying forever. Plus, I need that kind of education to be able to run a business in the future."

Her father took a deep breath and cupped her cheek with his hand. "I've never said no to anything you asked for, but for this one time... I want you to listen to me."

Nivri looked up at her father. "Daddy, please don't sound so sad. You know I'll do anything for you."

"I know, my child. Promise me you will come back to Hyderabad after you are done with your education and think about getting married."

She smiled looking at her father. "Okay, I will think about getting married, but I want to discuss my career with you."

"I have a better idea." Her father winked.

"Really? And what is that?"

"What if you get married to a guy capable of running what I built? Then you'll need to discuss your career with that person."

"What's your point, Dad?" The hair on the back of her neck raised up almost in anticipation. She remembered what her grandma had told her the day she arrived.

"I'll cut to the chase. I have someone in mind who I think is a good match for you, and he is coming back from a business trip in a few hours. I want you to meet him tomorrow."

"What? No."

"Yes. I want you to meet Kishore tomorrow. He has been extremely successful and is a good man... he is the one I want you to marry."

"Dad... not happening. Not him. Never. I will *not* meet him." She wanted to scream, but she kept her voice low, not wanting to agitate her dad and his heart condition.

"Nivri, I've made the decision, and I have invited their family to join us for dinner here. The choice is yours, but you will meet him if you don't want me to feel insulted in front of everyone."

"Dad... please... you've never forced me into doing anything... why are..."

"Yes, I've never done it so try to understand why I am having to do that now." Her father's expression was stone cold.

"Daddy, I like..." She wanted to tell him about Avinash. Tell her father about the budding relationship, but he cut her off.

"No more discussions. He will be here tomorrow. I hope I can count on you to let me hold my head high every step of the way." Her father was not ready to budge, and when she looked at him in silence, he nodded and walked away. Unlike every other time she was upset, he had been the one to comfort her.

Chapter 16

Nivri was miserable. There was no other way to describe how she felt about everything that was going on. She lay in bed later that night, angry and upset at the same time. She was so relieved to see Avinash's name on her phone screen, but she could barely understand what he was saying due to a bad connection. He sent a message after multiple failed calls that he was at a place with no cell phone coverage, and that he would call her as soon as he was back.

Dinner was a quiet affair especially with Nivri and her father ignoring each other while her mom and grandma chatted discussing the party details for the following night like there was no tension in the room. She ate her food and went to her bedroom to read a book for longer than usual hoping Avinash would call. She didn't believe in throwing tantrums, so she didn't fight what her father as saying.

She knew her father would want only the best for her, but she was torn between being sad and angry. She was unhappy with her father about how he had expected her to consider marrying a man he knew she hated as a child. The fact that her father didn't let her talk and tell him about Avinash upset her more.

Her father was her best friend, her rock, and yet he chose to take the tone he did, and she couldn't get over it. She only wished she could talk to Avinash just for a few minutes—not that she would have complained to him about her dad, but she wanted to tell Avinash about him meeting her parents. She was just happy falling in love but had not thought about marriage because it was too early.

Nivri couldn't remember when she fell asleep, but when she woke up, she could hear a lot of commotion from the backyard and almost cringed. She moved slowly reaching for her phone but nothing from Avinash. She threw her phone aside and lay in bed dreading how the rest of her day would go with the entire household prepping for a party that she was not looking forward to attending.

She was tempted to leave the house and come back after the party or fake a sickness and never leave her room—anything that would keep her from facing her childhood nemesis. She couldn't understand why he was willing to 'meet' her.

An arranged marriage?

Nivri had not given a lot of thought about marriage, at least not in recent times. She looked up at the ceiling, her eyes following the dark wood beams on the ceiling as she wondered where her relationship with Avinash was going.

Her heart drummed a parade at the memory of his beautiful face and loving eyes. Avinash had seen her low points and yet showed no annoyance with how she panicked on the plane. They shared the passion for educating underprivileged children, and she was ready to take a step toward a forever with him.

The creaking sound of the heavy door on her room interrupted her thoughts. She saw her grandma step into her room with a mug of steaming hot liquid.

"Nani, you forgot to knock," she grumbled as she rolled out of bed to put her arms around the older woman.

"I knocked... you didn't hear because you were lost in your own sweet world."

"I was not."

Her grandma handed her the mug and sat on the plush chair by Nivri's bed. "I'm surprised you didn't run away to your treehouse."

Nivri pressed her lips together and shook her head. She had gone to the treehouse after her argument with her father, and the entire room—the sheets, everything—smelled of Avinash and reminded her of his warmth. She couldn't bear the idea of longing for him and not being with him. She took a sip of the coffee her grandma brought for her and kept her eyes lowered. She knew why her grandma was in her room.

"Nivrithi, look at me." Nivri knew she was in trouble when her grandma addressed her by her full name. She slowly lifted her eyes to meet her grandma's loving ones.

"I want you to meet Kishore tonight, and you will not argue about it."

"But, Grandma... there is no..."

Her grandma interrupted her. "I know you like someone else, but tonight, you will meet Kishore because even if you don't get married to him, you will be working with him."

"What? Working with him? No way."

"Yes, you will be... your father is so impressed with what Kishore has done, he wants to invest in his company."

"What does he do that has impressed Daddy so much?"

"Why are you *not* so impressed with him?" Her grandma laughed.

"I just couldn't stand that guy growing up." She shrugged.

"You are all grown up now... maybe you will find him impressive."

"It doesn't matter if I am impressed with him, Nani, I'm not interested in him. I like someone else," she blurted.

"Oh... why didn't you tell Daddy that?"

"Your son... did not let me talk... his tone was so rude." She snarled.

Her grandma shook her head. "I think he wants you to meet Kishore. He would prefer you get married to him..."

Nivri didn't let her grandmother continue. "Nani, listen to me. I can't stand that guy. He's an asshole."

"No. He is a good boy."

"He tortured and annoyed me so much," she said, gritting her teeth.

"You weren't really a meek goat, were you?" her grandma retorted.

"I was only fighting back... I had to stand up to such bullies."

"He was never a bully, and you were the one who started it all."

"What? I did not."

"Yes, you did. Remember the time when you faked getting hurt when he barely touched you. Kishore got into a lot of trouble that day."

"Nani, it doesn't matter... I'm not..." her voice trailed off when her mother stepped into her bedroom.

"Hi, Ma."

"Nivri, why are you behaving so badly? You know very well you should not be stressing your father like this."

"Will you all take a chill pill? Why are you so freaked out about this and getting overly dramatic?"

"I am going to say this, and you are not going to like it. We want you to get married to Kishore because he is perfect for you."

"Have you all lost your mind? You guys are forcing me into a marriage when you know how much I despise that guy?"

"Grow up, Nivri. Just because you didn't get along well as kids, it doesn't mean you'll be the same way." Her mom was getting agitated.

"I like someone else, Mom. I wish you guys had given me the choice to pick the man I want to be with."

Her mother looked at her for a long moment. "Who is this person, and why are we hearing about him now?"

"I... I met him on the plane, and I like him."

"Do you want to marry him? This man you met less than a week back? Is this man even real? Are you making up stories to avoid meeting Kishore?" Her mom's tone was blunt.

"No, I am not, and it's too soon to think about marriage. I've only known him for a few days, but I..."

"Will he come talk to us? Bring his parents to meet us?"

"He is away, and I haven't talked to him in..."

Her mother cut her off. "You see the problem. You are disregarding a good match based on some feelings you have for this person you met a few days ago."

"Don't try to downplay what I feel, Mom. I love him."

Her grandma and mom both looked surprised but did not say anything.

"Are you ready to marry that man then?" Her mom asked after a long awkward silence.

"I want to know more about who he is and what his family is before…" Her voice trailed off when her mother shook her head.

"What you feel is gratitude for this man. What if he turns out to be from a family of murderers?"

"Stop being dramatic, Ma." Nivri knew her mom had a point. She knew nothing about Avinash, but everything about him felt right.

"Now, you stop being dramatic and dress up for the party tonight. I will have someone bring you the dress I had this designer make for you."

"How long have you guys been planning this?"

"Not long." Her mom smiled.

"But you conveniently had a dress made for the occasion for me?"

Her mom walked over to where Nivri stood, growling at the two women she loved to death. "I had ordered it for Diwali. I was going to send it to you to wear in New York."

"I still haven't decided if I even want to meet him, let alone consider him as a match."

"You will, Nivri. You will do what it takes for your father to save his face. We can think about what you decide about Kishore after the party. Be nice to him."

Nivri cursed not believing the sequence of events.

Chapter 17

Later that evening, Nivri stood looking at her reflection and smiled deviously. She was going to be a good daughter and help her parents host the party, but she was going to do it her way. She looked at the beautiful pink designer outfit that lay folded on the bed. She adjusted her curls into a partial ponytail behind her head and adjusted the red, silk saree that she had paired with a sequin gold cropped blouse that was an inner layer of her designer outfit.

Nivri chose to wear a saree and skip all the jewelry her mom had set out for her. The chain that Avinash had given her, she unhooked it and put it close to her heart inside her fitted blouse. She knew if she had one piece of jewelry on, her mom would make her wear more.

She wore a simple outfit refusing to give in to the pressure. She kept looking at her phone for messages or calls from Avinash and wondered why he hadn't called. She had thought to call him a few hours ago and decided not to. She knew he was away on work and didn't want to disturb him.

"Nivri… they are here… are you…" Her mom's words were lost in a gasp.

"What are you wearing? Why didn't you wear that dress?" Her mom was unhappy.

"Ma, that dress was so uncomfortable. I like this red saree."

"Whose saree is this?"

Nivri smiled. "It's Nani's. I borrowed it from her closet. Don't tell her."

"Nivri, what are you trying to do?"

"Ma, let's go, we don't want to be late," Nivri urged her mom, quickly walking past her toward the bedroom door.

"Nivri, stop."

Nivri stopped just before stepping out of her room and turned to look at her mother. Her mother walked over to where Nivri stood and cupped her cheek with her hand.

"Always remember that Daddy and I want the best for you. Just because he raised his voice, doesn't mean he doesn't love you. Your father has been miserable since yesterday."

Nivri smiled, batting away tears. "I know, Mom. I love you guys, too. I'll go talk to Daddy first."

"Be nice to Kishore... he is a very good guy."

"I'll be nice as long as he is nice to me. How many people did you and Daddy invite?"

"Just Kishore's family and ours. They are a big family just like ours. Be sure to say hi to everyone before you go talk to Kishore."

Nivri scrunched her nose. "Mom, how much time do you think I will be spending with Bunny... Kishore."

"Don't call him Bunny. I am told that's one thing he doesn't like to be called anymore."

"Good to know, Mom." Nivri smiled a mischievous thought crossing her mind.

"Take your time to know him well, sweetheart. You guys can go to the village fair that's happening in the nearby village if you want to hang out and talk."

"Ma, I will not be going to any village fair with him. Don't get your hopes up." Nivri almost snarled at her mom.

"Okay, fine. Let's go."

Nivri walked gingerly down the stairs smiling at the family who was gathered at the lower part of the ancestral home. She scanned the room for others, specifically Bunny aka Kishore, but didn't spot anyone other than her dad's cousins and their families. She spent time talking to everyone as her mom led to the far end of the main party area to where a small group had formed, and she instantly recognized everyone at the large sit-out area.

The first person she hugged was her grandma. "Thank you for letting me borrow your saree."

"You look beautiful, Nivri." Her grandma kissed her on her forehead.

"You look hotter, Nani." Nivri kissed her grandma on her cheek before walking to where her dad stood almost fighting back tears.

"Daddy, I'm sorry I yelled at you," she whispered as she put her arms around him.

"I love you, sweetheart. You look so beautiful." Her dad planted a kiss on her temple.

She turned to look at the man standing next to her dad and smiled. It was Kishore's dad, who was also her father's business advisor and friend.

"Gopal uncle, how are you?" She smiled hugging the older man.

"I am doing very well, Nivri. We are so happy to see you after such a long time," the older man said smiling and called out to his wife who was standing a few feet away talking to another family friend. "Deepa, look Nivri is all grown up."

The woman ended her conversation and walked toward Nivri, smiling. "Look at you, Nivri. You look like a model."

"Deepa aunty, you are so sweet." Nivri laughed, hugging her.

The older woman cupped her hand over Nivri's cheek and looked at Nivri's mother. "Reetu, Give Nivri to me, please."

Nivri understood the underlying meaning of her ask but smiled and stayed quiet. Thankfully, her mom had a better sense of humor than her. "Deepa, take her. She has been such an unruly child. I've been meaning to put her up for adoption."

Nivri laughed. "Deepa aunty, how is Bunny doing?"

Kishore's mother let out a soft gasp and started laughing. "Nivri, I totally forgot you were the one who gave him that name. None of us call him by that name. We were asked not to... not after high school, I think."

Nivri smiled looking around wondering where the guy who was to be considered as her match was, so she could actually call him by his nickname, to his face.

"Gopal, where is Kishore?"

"He was here just a few minutes ago. Oh, there he is...." Kishore's father pointed to a tall silhouette of a man walking down the path to the garden, the screen of his phone illuminated against his ear.

"Gopal, can you have him join us, please? That boy is obsessed with his work." His mother shook her head.

"It's okay, I know he was expecting an important call," his father said and added, "Nivri, why don't you guys go talk in the garden. You have a lot of catching up to do. You two haven't seen each other after Kishore left for the United States for college."

"That's a wonderful idea, Gopal," her father cheered, and Nivri had a tough time stopping herself from rolling her eyes.

"Nivri, you guys should check out the village fair. I heard the street food is killer," her mom called out as she started walking away from the outdoor patio toward her childhood nemesis. She kept her eyes on the lit-up phone screen as she walked and stopped in her tracks when her phone started to ring. She had her phone tucked at the waistband of her saree skirt.

Nivri's lips stretched into a smile when she saw Avinash was calling.

Chapter 18

Nivri answered the phone in a flash. "Hey, where have you been? I've waiting to talk to you."

"Me, too, love. I was stuck in a place with no signal and couldn't call sooner. I missed you."

"I missed you, too." She felt a lump form in her throat.

"What are you doing?"

She let out a chuckle. "I am about to talk to a guy who my mom and dad think will make a good husband for me."

"Oh, interesting."

"You were off the grid, and my folks got impatient," she teased.

"Yeah? Who is the lucky guy?" He laughed.

"Not funny, Avinash. If there is one guy I can't stand, it's him. Oh, this is the guy who spit gum in my hair... remember I told you... Bunny."

"Interesting... you don't like him, and you are going to talk to him with intentions of marrying him."

"Yikes no, not going to think of him that way... not happening."

"Do you think of me that way?"

Nivri knew what he meant and smiled. "Like what? I don't know what you mean."

He chuckled. "This is not something I should be asking you on the phone, but do you think I'll make a good husband?"

Her breath got trapped in her throat. "Avinash..."

"I love you, Nivri, and what started off as a funny coincidence turned into life-changing moments for me. You can be mad at me all you want, but I want you for the rest of my life."

She let out a sob, happy tears rolling down her cheeks. "You picked such an odd time and place to tell me this. Why don't I see this guy who is standing there waiting to talk to me and then you come get me. We can go to the village fair."

"Nivri..." His voice was gravelly. "Come to me, baby."

Nivri was standing a few feet from the man who she was supposed to talk to, and he hadn't seen her yet. She debated if she should walk away and pretend like she never found Kishore and go see Avinash. "Where are you, Avinash?"

"Right here."

"Where?" She turned away from the man and looked at the mansion.

"Baby, I love you... don't be mad."

"Why will I be mad?" Nivri asked and saw he had ended the call. She cursed, and before she could dial him again, she heard his voice. She looked in the direction of the house expecting him to walk to her from the house, but when he called out to her again, is when she realized his voice was coming from behind her.

A sudden thought crossed her mind, and his last words rang in her head as she turned to look at the man she was set up to meet by her parents. She let out a gasp when the tall silhouette was starting to be more and more familiar as he moved closer to her.

"Baby," Avinash said stepping under the dim light in the garden.

"Avi... Avinash." She let out a sob, and all her questions and confusions melted, and she gave in to the need to hug him. She closed the gap between them and threw her hands around him.

"Where the heck did you disappear to?" she growled.

Avinash laughed, planting a kiss on the top of her head as she sobbed into his chest, happy tears staining his shirt.

"Sweetheart, before you get mad at me, let me..." his voice trailed off when she pulled back abruptly and swept her fingers over his cheek causing a burn to start.

"Why didn't you tell me who you were, idiot?" she barked, throwing her arms around him again.

He laughed, his breath warm on her cheek as he lifted her off the ground.

"How long have you known?" she demanded.

"The moment I saw you, I knew who you were."

She slapped him gently on his arm. "Why didn't to tell me?"

"I was hoping to avoid getting slapped, but I guess there was no avoiding it. We picked up where we left off years ago."

"You deserve more than just that for putting me through a crappy day." She sunk her teeth into his neck making him hard.

Avinash tightened his hold on her. "Baby, you do that one more time, and I'll bite you back."

"I dare you to…" she groaned, taking a bite into his ear.

She felt him shudder and swore she felt his desire for her over her bare belly as he placed her feet back on the ground and took a step back. "You look beautiful in a saree."

"I would have worn a designer outfit if I knew it was you I was meeting." She smiled, and his lips came down on hers in the most devouring kiss she waited for all day. His lips were hungry, but he pulled back when she was about to get lost in him.

Her eyes fluttered open as he let her go, and they widened in surprise as he stepped back to go down on one knee, holding a diamond ring in his hand. "Nivri, my name is Avinash Kishore Sangha aka Bunny. I love you and promise to cherish and protect you forever. Will you marry me?"

Nivri laughed, covering her mouth with her hands. "Yes... Bunny, I love you, too."

She gave him her hand, and he slipped the ring on her finger. It fit perfectly. He stood up as she brought her hand closer to her. "It's beautiful."

"And if you are wondering why I was off the grid, I was having this made by a jeweler whose family has been making wedding rings for our family for decades."

"This is the perfect size, too," she said admiring her engagement ring.

"I measured it when you were sleeping... in the treehouse." He brushed his lips over hers making her smile.

"Should we tell our parents we are going to the village fair and get out of here?" She winked, tightening her hold on him.

"Why don't we tell them we are engaged and put them out of their misery. I'm sure they are on pins and needles knowing how much we enjoyed each other's company in high school."

"Yeah, let's tell them and you, Mr. Husband, you are going to pay for all the crap you put me through," she warned, winking at him.

"Bring it on, baby. It'll only make me want you more."

Chapter 19

Nivri held her hand up smiling into the camera as Avinash held her to him to take a picture of the two of them.

"What do you think their reaction would be if we tell them we met even before they set us up to meet?" Nivri laughed looking at the picture of them on the camera screen.

Avinash shook his head. "Let's not... let them think they set us up, and we decided to get married. Everyone will get a kick out of it."

"I love that idea... I made such a stink about not meeting you because I loved someone else, my mom will confirm her theory about my made-up love story." Nivri laughed.

Avinash laughed. "My mom and dad will be shocked that I proposed to you the moment I saw you, especially when they think I just got back from New York."

"Did they not know you were in India?"

"Nope. We wrapped up early in New York, and it feels like I got on that plane at the last minute... just to meet you." He kissed her cheek.

"Why didn't you tell we met before?"

"My family is still traumatized from my cousin eloping and not having an arranged marriage. They are fine, but... I'll tell you more later." He laughed.

"Our engagement news will go viral on the internet." She laughed, hugging him.

"Okay, I am going to send them this picture and tell them I am taking my fiancée to the village fair?"

"Sure."

Avinash typed the message and hit send on the message to their parents. Moments passed, and Avinash and Nivri waited staring at the phone for a reply, but what they did not expect was a loud cheer from the house like everyone in the building was cheering for them.

The next moment, fireworks started rising in the sky, and both their phones started buzzing with congratulatory messages.

"Let's get out of here before they come to get us to join their fun." Avinash took her hand in his.

Nivri pulled him back and stood rooted to her spot. "Avinash, make me yours once and for all."

He smiled, framing her face with his hands. "You are mine, Nivri... forever."

She nodded smiling and reached for his chain she had put away on her chest. He smiled at her when she pulled it out of her fitted blouse and handed it to him. "I don't need a ceremony. I'm yours."

He kissed her on her forehead and clipped the necklace around her neck and bent down to kiss the pendant that fell on her chest before standing up to brush his lips over hers. "Let's go, baby."

"I don't want to go to the village fair," she whined, following him down the path to the fields.

"I know, me neither." He chuckled, leading her toward the treehouse.

"Just where I wanted to go." She laughed, breaking into a slow run to keep up with him. They climbed up the spiral staircase and crashed on the mattress as soon as the doors opened, laughing. He pulled her close to him, his hand running over the bare skin on her midriff sending waves of electricity through her.

"I have something to share with you... you will be the first one to know." He kissed her cheek.

"What?" She placed her hand in his cheek enjoying the roughness of his stubble.

"The New York deal, we got it... Nash Technologies is now a true global company. We've expanded to the Americas."

"Oh my God... that's awesome!"

"Will you let me be your co-passenger when you go back to New York?"

She nodded, fighting back happy tears. "Avinash, I can't believe this... I am the luckiest woman in this world."

"You are my lucky charm because the moment I laid eyes on you, the love of my life landed in my lap, literally." He laughed, and she smiled remembering how she sat on his lap when she thought the plane was going to crash.

"Will you really go with me to New York?"

"Yes, love." He kissed her forehead and started trailing his lips lower.

"Will you stay with me until I graduate?"

"Yes." His sucked on the delicate skin on her neck making her squirm. The hand at her waist went up to cup the curve of her breast. "When I saw you come down those stairs in the red saree, I wanted to throw you over my shoulder and take you away from the party, and I was glad I got that call to distract me."

"Will you..." Her question turned into a gasp when she felt his lips on the bare skin of her belly before his teeth sunk into the skin above her belly button.

"Baby, I want you so bad... I can't wait anymore." He gripped the pleats of the saree and pulled them out of the waistband.

She rolled over onto her tummy breaking the contact from his lips. "Unhook the buttons on my blouse, it's getting harder to breathe when you kiss me like that."

He chuckled running his palm over her back, his fingers following her curves, making her wiggle her bottom, giggling. She let out a squeal when he smacked her bottom before reaching for the hooks on the back of her blouse. He put part of his weight on her from behind and unhooked one button at a time followed by a kiss on the exposed skin.

Every kiss on her back sent waves of new pleasure through her body. She could feel every nerve ending turn raw, and the anticipation for the ultimate pleasure grew as he trailed slow, purposeful kisses down her back.

She let out a squeal when he picked her off the mattress like a rag doll to flip her over to face him. He ran his hand over her shoulders, pulling the fitted blouse off her chest exposing her well- rounded breasts. Her nipples were tight, and he gently tapped each one making a wave a moisture surge at the apex of her thighs.

Avinash looked down at her, her golden skin glowing against the red of the silk fabric that was still wrapped around her hips, and the yellow gold chain with his name on it sparkled. "I'll make you mine, tonight."

"I'm yours, forever." She pulled on the tab at her waist that kept the skirt of her saree intact and wiggled her hips to expose the bright pink lacey panties she had on.

He pulled back to unbutton his shirt, and she sat up and reached for his shirt like she couldn't bear the wait anymore. He kissed her for every button she removed, and when she ripped apart the last one, his mouth crashed into hers, his tongue plunging into her warmth.

Unlike the other times, this time he was eager to touch her, feel her, and she gave in to his desires. "Don't make me wait."

"I promise you every ounce of happiness and pleasure in this world." His voice was hoarse, and he pulled back to shed his dress pants and boxers with them.

When he came back, she reached out to stroke his hardness while kissing him, enjoying the heat and the throbbing against her palm. As she stroked him, he kissed her delicate skin, and when he groaned into her skin taking a little nip over the spot, she came undone. And when she felt the warmth of his release on her hand, it gave her immense pride—that she was the reason for his pleasure.

Avinash reached for a tissue from the side table and wiped her hand clean before gently pushing her back onto the mattress. "I want you now, sweetheart. Are you ready for me?"

Nivri smiled, nodding at him, feeling the jitters with every passing moment. He stroked her folds with his steely thickness a few times before introducing the pink tip to her folds.

Her body tensed with the initial pang of burn, but when he leaned into her kissing and nibbling her skin as he inched into her, the burn started to soothe away, and something new took over. Her eyes rolled shut unable to handle the intensity of the moment. When he hit the deepest point, she felt whole, and the emptiness she never realized she had, melted away.

He buried his face into her neck and built a rhythm igniting new sensations and emotions. She held him tightly, her arms wrapped around him, her fingers fisted in his hair. When he hit deeper and deeper with every stroke, she felt the need to explode into a million pieces unable to handle the pleasure.

"Come for me, baby!" It was an order, and that did it. She felt the waves of electricity buzz through her, and in the background, she saw the fireworks that were lit just at that moment. She felt every tiny piece of that fireball run through her taking her over the edge.

She called out his name in sheer pleasure, and he groaned, pulling out of her to pour out his warmth over her belly and collapsing onto her side, pulling her over him. Their bodies were slick with sweat, and the room had reached fever pitch from their passionate lovemaking.

"Avinash, I love you."

"I love you with all my heart, baby. Be mine, and I will give you the world."

Epilogue

Four months later...

"You look beautiful, sweetheart," Nivri's father said fighting back tears.

It was Nivri's and Avinash's wedding night. The ceremony was about to begin, and her mother and father came into her suite to see her before they headed to the wedding pavilion to start the wedding rituals.

"I agree... you are the most beautiful bride in this whole world." Her mom air-kissed her.

"Thank you, Mom." She smiled knowing how biased the mother of the bride could be about her daughter.

"Okay, sweetheart, we have to go, but Nani will be here with you until we come back to take you," her father told her like he forgot she had grown past seven years of age.

She smiled at him. "I love you, Daddy. Love you more, Ma."

"See, my daughter finally confessed she loves me more." Her mother laughed, and they left the bridal suite.

Nivri turned to look at her grandma who she knew was having a tough time containing her excitement. "I love you the most, Nani."

Her grandma smiled at her and stood up to walk over to where Nivri sat strapped in a beautiful silk saree and weighed down by gold ornaments.

Nivri looked up at her grandma. "Nani, what's wrong?"

"Nivri... are you happy with this wedding?"

Nivri laughed in response. "I'm getting married in less than thirty minutes. Interesting question. Why do you ask?"

"When you came to India for Diwali, you told me you liked this boy, and then when you met Kishore, you liked him, and everything happened so fast. A woman's first love is very deep and strong and will never die... I hope you have no regrets about your decision."

Nivri smiled and stood up to hug her grandma. "Okay, if you promise never to repeat what I am about to tell you, I'll let you in on a secret."

Her grandma nodded vigorously and leaned closer. "The guy I met on the plane who held me when I had my panic attack and drove me home all the way from Hyderabad, and the man I am about to marry... same person."

"What? No. You told me his name is Avinash." Her grandma was surprised.

"Yes, Nani... Avinash Kishore is his full name, and that's why his company is called Nash Technologies."

"Oh. Why didn't you tell anyone that?"

"Do you remember the look on Daddy's face when he saw the picture of him and me that night? You saw it live, I had to watch it on video." Nivri laughed.

Her grandma laughed, wiping the edge of her eyes. "I remember that night. You know the doctor said his heart health has also improved a lot after you and Kishore decided to get married."

"I know." Nivri winked.

"So, no one knows?" Her grandma's voice held surprise.

"Only Bunny and me and now you."

"I'm so happy to hear that and... it is very sweet that you still call him Bunny."

Nivri smiled. "I gave him that name when we were kids, and he actually likes it."

"Does he take good care of you, Nivri?"

"Again, the timing is way off for your question, but, yes. He does... He took such good care of me when he stayed with me after I went back to New York," Nivri blurted.

"He stayed with *you*?" Her grandma caught on to the minor detail.

"Okay... yes. He did. We were an engaged couple, Nani."

Her grandma shook her head. "Don't tell me any more."

Nivri laughed hugging the elderly woman. "I love him, and he loves me to death, and that's all matters. We are going to go on our honeymoon and then work together on merging Daddy's company with Bunny's."

"What honeymoon, didn't you already have one in New York?" Her grandma teased.

Nivri shook her head. "Honeymoon is honeymoon... it's special."

"So, you had a love marriage when we all think we arranged it."

Nivri though for a moment. "*Arranged Love*, Nani."

Her grandma kissed her on her cheek. "Bless you, my child. All I want now is to hold my great-grandchildren in my hands... before I go."

"Nice try, Nani. You are not going anywhere. Avinash... Kishore and I have a lot to do before we have a baby."

Nivri spent precious moments in that bridal suite with her grandma until she was ushered toward the wedding pavilion to ceremoniously tie the knot with the love of her life. She walked down the path lined with lights and flowers surrounded by family and friends, happiness overflowing her heart. Just when she thought she couldn't be happier, her eyes locked with the man she loved deeply, and her heart started to sing. She knew at that moment, all she needed was his smile that lit up his eyes, and that look always sent her heart on a rampage.

Later that night, after the reception, it was way past midnight by the time they returned to their wedding suite.

"Guess what my Nani asked me today like thirty minutes before the ceremony started?"

"What?" He frowned.

"She asked me if I was still in love with the guy I met on the plane."

He chuckled. "What did you tell her?"

She smiled looking up at him. "Our marriage is *Arranged Love*."

Avinash smiled and led her to their suite and held the door open for her. "After you, Mrs. Sangha."

"Thank you, Mr. Bunny Sangha." She laughed and threw her arms around him when he shut the door and pushed her back into the wall, his lips going to his favorite spot on her neck.

"You were probably a vampire in your past life," she laughed enjoying the delectable pleasure from the way he sucked on her skin.

"I would probably eat you for every meal if I were a vampire," he growled, sending vibrations that triggered thrills between her legs.

Nivri took in a deep breath trying to contain the pleasure as he unzipped her dress, pushing aside the soft material, possessively cupping one breast with his hand and taking another into his mouth. She moaned taking in every sensation, touch, and kiss.

When he picked her up to crash their melded bodies onto the bed, the flowers on the bed flew all around them along with their clothes, and when they consummated their marriage, she knew that one of the best decisions was to get on that plane from New York to surprise her family. She was happy and thankful for the surprise life gave her, and she couldn't ask for more but to be in Avinash's arms, forever.

***** The End *****

AUTHOR'S NOTE

Thank you for reading *Arranged Love*. I hope you enjoyed reading Nivri and Avinash's love story. Thank you for being part of their beautiful journey.

I would like to ask you to rate/review this book on Amazon and Goodreads as it will help me know what you, my readers, would like to see in future stories.

Read on for a sneak peek of my new release, **The Rule Breaker!**

Thank you,
P.G. Van

Email: pgvanpublish@gmail.com

New Release

@Amazon: https://smarturl.it/TheRuleBreaker

The Rule Breaker has it all—stunning good looks, fame, fortune, and screaming fans. The notorious lead singer is the brains behind one of the biggest bands in the country. He has the power to mesmerize millions. Can she withstand his charm and undeniable magnetism?

She was one of his adoring fans but not after what happened five years back. A conversation he didn't care to remember and one she cannot forget.

The last thing she expected when she agreed to join his band on a tour was getting close to him, too close for comfort.

He is the rule breaker, and she could not let him break something so precious—**her heart**.

BOOKS BY P.G.Van

Check out my Amazon page for the full list of books:

Made in the USA
Coppell, TX
02 June 2020